RUNNING

& other stories

Makhosazana Xaba

modjaji books

Publication © Modjaji Books 2013

Text © Makhosazana Xaba 2013

P O Box 385, Athlone, 7760, South Africa

modjaji.books@gmail.com

www.modjajibooks.co.za

ISBN 978-1-920590-16-1

Cover artwork and lettering by Carla Kreuser

Book and cover design by Natascha Mostert

Author photograph by Zed Xaba

Printed and bound by Creda Communications, Cape Town

Set in Garamond

Dedicated to my mother
Glenrose Nomvula Xaba
(22.06.1929 – 27.05.2011)

and her two sisters
Grace Thembani Mashaba (17.10.1932 – 08.12.1996)
and **Doreen Mildred "Twana" Dlamini** (21.03.1936 – 29.06.1991),
the daughters of Nokubekezela Mkhabela and Alban Mbatha.

OMama abathathu, oNdabezitha.

Contents

Foreword

I am delighted to be writing the Foreword to Makhosazana Xaba's debut short story collection after two groundbreaking poetry volumes, *These hands* and *Tongues of their mothers*. Reading her poems over the years has felt simultaneously like a homecoming and a breakthrough. The short stories between the covers of the book you hold before you offered me something of that familiar feeling. Sometimes I realised that I knew something that I had not quite grasped until the point at which one of Xaba's characters pulled back the delicate onion-skin layers.

She revises the iconic South African short story "The Suit" twice in this collection. Although the opening and closing stories are conventionally thought of as *framing* what lies between them, Xaba's altered suits present questions, not assurance. In conversation with fellow writers Zukiswa Wanner and Siphiwo Mahala, who have also taken their imaginations to Can Themba's story, infusing it with different life, Xaba's rewritings also invite us to think about the very project she is engaged in. It is not simply that she gives voice to women *differently* to Themba, Mahala and even Wanner before her. What does it mean to voice women differently? What does it mean to imagine women's stories, desires and fears in ways that are free and freeing? Makhosazana Xaba answers this question over and over again in the short stories in *Running and other stories*.

While readers will recognise themselves in some of the stories, tastes and mental geographies mapped by Xaba, there is much to discover and delight in. What does a revolutionary woman think about in the middle of a historic moment she is part of fashioning? "Running" interweaves the sobering and the delightful to present one sort of answer to this question. I thought of the narrator in this story as someone who might be friends with the speaker in Xaba's poem, "these hands".

Who is that girl that survives the impossible, seeming hopeless from the outside? "Prayers" broke my heart in as many ways as it gave me hope, listening to a little girl whose life is more complicated than any child's should be, brought fully to life by a writer who captures the cadences of a girl's voices perfectly. Although my life has never been anything like Refiloe's, I remembered some of her feelings about a girl's body growing into a woman's body, while life happens speedily around her, from another life. Zodwa, Qhamukile and Bhekiwe hold hands across the two stories "Inside" and "The trip". They never meet in the stories, yet they live in the same world, same city of the imagination. I am sure I see glimpses of them in my town, my friends, my own home.

I chuckled with sheer delight as Xaba played games with plot and the very architecture of what we expect from the genre of short stories in "The odds of Dakar". The genius in this particular story blew me away.

The collection is also haunted by the same fears and threats that beleaguer all women who live in a society where patriarchal violence is endemic. The worlds Xaba creates in these short stories are courageous; they are also playful and brimming with curiosity.

The stories leak into one another here because Xaba's girl/women characters speak unfashionably, think for themselves, re-arrange the world with their chosen expressions of desire. This is a collection that unapologetically centres women's voices and experiences, at the same time as pushing the boundaries of what this ordinarily means. Xaba has never been content in her writing to simply present the unconventional , she re-imagines the very notion of what we expect from a short story, from a woman, from a girl. In *Running and other stories*, she raises the bar on what is conceivable for creative writers and imaginative readers.

Written with the generosity of a novelist and the precision of a poet, *Running and other stories* is a gem of a collection. I am thrilled it now exists in the world.

Pumla Dineo Gqola
University of the Witwatersrand
30 January 2013

Behind *The Suit*

MY DARLING DAUGHTER,

To be terminally ill and write from a hospital bed at the age of eighty is a tad risky; the tendency to romanticise abounds. To write a farewell missive to a daughter you barely know borders on the duplicitous. So I will stick to the bones, a frame and form for you to hold me in should events in your life ever conspire to draw you close to such proclivity.

Your life experiences will definitely give you the coverings, and, if you are lucky even the blood to flow through flesh. You probably have to wait till you are sixty, perhaps fifty, if you are lucky, to gather the marrow to fill these bones. Filling in the marrow is your choice, unlike the coverings that will hit you again and again, just because you are my daughter. No choices there.

Bare bones number one: my side of your family tree. I don't know what your mother told you before passing away, as she would not speak to me about such matters. My mother's name was Hloniphekile. As a designated healer, five generations down the line, she was given this special name. Respectable – she sure was. Like most people in Johannesburg, her father had come from Natal as a mineworker. He was a proud Zulu man of the Mbatha clan. He died a sad death in the bowels of the earth digging for gold, something he would never use even if he had known how. They say his body was never found, a fact that has remained a source of great consternation to the whole family.

My mother had just turned eighteen when her father died. He had brought her to Johannesburg to find work, leaving her younger siblings and mother in Natal. My mother always said she had her father to thank, because she doubted that her healing profession would have prospered had she remained in Natal. Needless to say, she never found a job she liked, and soon after her father's funeral her ancestors began to speak to her, turning her into the professional healer she was meant to be.

Hloniphekile – your grandmother – was also a very gifted communicator. Ancestors spoke through her. They taught her everything she knew about herbs, healing and disease. She never had to go for formal training, you know, the apprenticeship that many herbalists have to undergo. She was known all over Sophiatown. The sophisticates – teachers, nurses and journalists – came to consult her under the light of the stars, to protect their public image. The simple others were proud to consult her by day. I owe my education to her profession.

She was not meant to marry anyone, so I never knew my father, expect by name, Batsane Kgosidintsi, a Motswana from Botswana, known then as the Bechuanaland Protectorate. I was to be her only child. Your grandmother made sure that she raised me to believe in myself, and when life was hard, she solicited assistance from her ancestors. I had a protected childhood. I was happy. I was privileged in that I had everything I needed and asked for. Having no siblings to share with really felt like a privilege. Your grandmother was a very special woman, something I understood the full gravity of only in my mature years, when I began to be of the world, in a real sense.

I have fought with these nurses, mere girls really, so much while writing that I am surprised they continue to think that my writing can worsen my condition. What is the point of stopping me from living whatever life I can live when I have only a few days left? You'd swear I was insisting on playing soccer. I was discharged from the ICU a week ago. I am strong now. Strong enough to die with dignity holding me and fixing her loving eyes on me, like a mother holds a baby feeding at her breast.

Bare bones number two: how I met your mother. I have no doubt she told you about this, but my version of it matters too. So here goes. I resigned from *Zonk*, the newspaper, so I could leave the country like some of my colleagues and contemporaries. I needed to become who I could become. Your grandmother encouraged me to leave. She wanted me to be free. She said I belonged to the world, and not to her or Sophiatown. And she told me that the ancestors would look after me, wherever I am.

A day before my departure, she presided over a ceremony that I have lived to cherish. It flooded the path of my life with enchanting lights and curious scents. Once in Swaziland, I did what most of us did: I met your mother through political activities and we became friends, of the comradely sort.

We learned about the Sharpeville massacre on the evening we were meant to work together on some project in KwaHlatikhulu, a small town with a veneer of tranquillity. We drank more than we should have, contemplated the meaning of our lives in alcohol-induced verbosity, fell asleep in each other arms on the lounge floor, and comforted each other the only way we knew for the rest of the night. We each experienced our firsts: me with a woman and she with a black man. You, my darling angel, were to be the precious product of those firsts.

When you were born your mother said "your tan" was just what she had imagined, dark caramel. Philemon, my lover at the time, had been in Swaziland for three months. I told him about you a week after you were born. He felt betrayed. It so consumed him that his entire worldview changed. He began to make plans to emigrate to London. Those were such strange times. There were days when I doubted that that was *my* life. It had taken me two years to convince Philemon to leave Sophiatown and come and join me in Swaziland. And you, my angel, were seducing me in ways I never thought infants were capable of. I was falling in love with you every single day. If truth be told, you changed my life.

You will not believe what just happened. The Sister-in-Charge decided to "report" me to the matron "for the sake of my health". I am a journalist and I will write till I die, why they don't get that, I don't know. As I am not meant to stress myself and have refused to listen to their instructions (I wrote a lot yesterday as well), she thought it in my best interests to inform the matron on duty.

"Good evening, sir." She greeted me with a soft voice and a wide smile. I looked up to see a woman who could not be younger than 60, definitely close to retirement. Her navy blue uniform hugged her uncomfortably around her waist and her bust. Two buttons around the bust displayed some strain.

"I thought I should inform you in person, sir; I have told the nurses, including Sister-in-Charge, that you have my permission to write as many letters as your heart desires." I smiled and offered my hand. She smiled and gave me her back without another word. We needed none.

Bare bones number three: the truth I am not proud of. I have always been fascinated by how some events metamorphose as they take on a life of their own over time. This one in particular has never failed to astound me because of its origins – innocence, jest. A mere joke behind such a calamity!

To this day, in my mind I can see Philemon's face when he came to tell me about catching Matilda in the act. My mother called my name from the stoep of her "therapy room", a shack really, but that's what we called it. She had built it when I was just eight years old, insisting that her clients needed privacy.

"Mondli! Umuntu wakho!" That's how she always referred to Philemon – Mondli, your person – much to his chagrin. Philemon, what a complex human being!

He hated that about my mother, who did not think there was anything to be concerned about. In her view, the ancestors were content with us as lovers. When Phil entered my bedroom, he was breathing heavily, carrying a parcel in old newspaper, folded as neatly as only Phil could fold. It was the suit. I was shocked he had even remembered to bring it with him. But that was Phil. He thrived on detail.

Luck was on his side because that was a Monday I was not working. It was payback time for one of my colleagues who had been ill for some time, and in whose place I had worked. It was a Monday that gave pens permission to dance into numerous tomorrows.

I could see Philemon was very angry. I thought his anger was inappropriate, an overreaction and hypocritical, so I challenged him, joking.

"Make her suffer, Phil, make her feed the suit."

"What?"

For the first time he looked right into my eyes. He stopped rolling his left hand around his right thumb. As usual when he did this I wondered about how hot his thumb must feel. But it was the wrong moment to tease him.

"I said, make her suffer."

"But, what do you mean, 'make her feed the suit'?"

He had that smooth quiver on both sides of his mouth. I had come to know this quiver denoted extreme anger. The faster and less smooth these movements, the closer he approached rage.

Problem was, I didn't know what I was saying either. The words had simply tumbled out of my mouth without a second of pondering. A part of me wanted to say I was just joking, but another part of me I was surprised to find awake was busy cooking up a plan.

"Phil, you are angry, right?"

"Right."

"You want to punish her, humiliate her…"

He nodded. His eyes fixed on mine. Had Phil been thinking straight at that moment, he would have seen what he had come to call "the giveaway expression" on my face. I wanted to laugh my lungs out, but Phil was embroiled in his anger. Then his shoulders dropped a whole inch. A faint smile replaced the quiver at the sides of his lips.

"I like that idea. Hmmm, I like it very much."

He had a way of clapping his hands when he was excited about something, or when he had just had a bright spark cross his mind. It was a light clap, just one, often accompanied by one word "yes" or "awuzweke" or "ushwentshweni" or "okay", depending on the context and his mood. Imagine my shock when I heard that Phil had in fact followed through on my joke.

Phil could not find it in his heart to accept your arrival, my dark caramel angel. And he refused completely to talk about Matilda after her death. He found a way to move to London when you were six months old. He told me never to contact him again. Your mother left for New York soon after you started walking. She said your grandparents were wealthy, they were excited by the possibility of raising their granddaughter as a proper Jewish girl, and that you stood a chance of getting a much better education out there. Eighteen months after Phil left, I arrived in London. I began looking for him. Two months later, I learned his life had ended in the same way as Matilda's: suicide.

I remembered one of my mother's many sayings: all futures are bred in the bellies of their pasts. Your grandmother had told me that our ancestors had given Phil and I what we had. She transited to ancestorhood a month after I landed in London. I was told that she read the first letter that I wrote her after getting to London to all the neighbours, and kept telling them she was now ready to die because I was now safe from the cruelty of the police and the unforgiving Sophiatownians. I have never stopped wondering what she would have said about Phil's suicide.

I had no way of knowing then that I would live long enough to return home, let alone convey this narrative, and that it would be to you, in a missive like this. Deep down, I know it's better to leave this story behind. The only thing worth carrying forward is our correspondence, scanty as it may be. I am still keeping that very first missive you wrote to me when you started school. Remember that? In my heart, our communication looms larger that the mountains of uKhahlamba.

I wanted to name you Fakazile. Your mother would not hear of it, "for your own good". She said her Jewish family would have difficulty pronouncing that name. Go and find out what it means and honour it. That is, if you ever wish to come here and learn about the country that produced you and us.

The lights will be out soon. Pardon these gushy ruminations from an old man.

I remain,

Your loving Daddy
Mondliwesizwe Mbatha

Prayers

MY NAME IS Refiloe. I am thirteen years old. My sister Lesedi is four. My parents passed away last year. Papa went first, three months before Mme.

It all began in February last year, when Papa came back from the mines in Johannesburg. An ambulance dropped him right in front of our home, too ill to walk and talk. The driver of the ambulance spoke to Mme for a long time as the neybars helped carry Papa into the house. He told Mme how difficult it was to find our village because it is tucked away between two hills, and he is not used to driving in areas where there are no road signs. And the roads are very bad. What he didn't know is that the roads were once horrific. At least now they are wider and that makes it easier for cars, now two cars can stand alongside each other. This means that the road does not get used up too quickly, and on rainy days mud does not accumulate too fast, making them impassable.

I remember that day when a man came from the government offices to talk to all the elders in the village about the plans to improve the roads and install a water pump for our village that we could all use instead of going all the way to the river. Mme was delighted, so was I. We had a water tank that my father bought years ago, when I was seven. But in winter when there are no rains, we use up all the water and have to go to the river. I hate walking to the river in winter, it gets dark very early and the shadows of the hill make it so much colder than it really is. The river is right next to the foot of the hill, where it really freezes.

As I was saying, the ambulance driver complained to Mme. He said he had to stop many times asking people where to find Moosa's General Dealers, our main store. Apparently that was all my father could tell him because he was very ill and could not talk much. Although I was very sad to see Papa like that, I was relieved that he had come back home. As Mme kept telling us, "It's much better to die with your family, with love around you and prayers for your future life." Everyone thought Papa would pass away very soon after he arrived home. Many people now say Mme's love kept him alive.

Granny-next-door (her village nickname is very rude, Mme said we could just call her Granny-next-door) kept telling Mme that the reason Papa was staying alive for so long even when he was in such pain was because our ancestors were still paving the way for him in their land. Apparently there is a special way to be when one arrives in that land. She also said that although we could neither see nor hear Papa talk to them, she was sure it was happening because the ancestors speak in a language we cannot understand. I asked Mistress Maluleke about ancestors. She just said I must wait till I am older: "Understanding ancestors comes with age and maturity, child." Most old people in my village talk about ancestors a lot, but they don't want us present when they have these conversations.

Now back to Papa. He passed away six months after the ambulance dropped him off. Many neybars I heard talk to Mme said she was very brave to nurse him until his last day when the hospital could have taken care of him very well. But Mme had one belief; if the hospitals in Johannesburg had sent him home, our hospital in town couldn't do anything better. It's the longest time I remember spending with Papa. As a mining man he only came home for the Christmas and Easter holidays. There were years when he did not come during the Easter holidays because he had no money. One of those years was the year my sister was born. Mme said he had to buy extra food and so many baby clothes that he simply could not afford money to come home. Mme also said this was the life of all mining men in our village. They hardly ever saw their families because there is very little money paid to them. It takes a long time to dig gold, diamonds and coal from the stomach of the earth. Sometimes they could dig for months without finding even the smallest piece. The bosses paid the miners only when they dig enough gold and diamonds. Mme always prayed that Papa could find a job in a gold or diamond mine because the mining men were better paid in those mines. Papa was in a coal mine that was notorious for paying very little because South Africa did not sell coal to other countries.

I hope I have not bored you with this long beginning, full of recent history. Mistress Maluleke said I must "paint pictures" when I tell this story. Our lives depend on it.

So here is what I should have started with. My school is called Lesedi Primary School, LPS for short. It's one of the schools built by the former President Mandela. It's big and beautiful. It is so beautiful it looks lost among the village houses. In this village, many children born that year were named Lesedi, just like my sister. I will not say much about our school. Mistress Maluleke will be able to tell you much more about it than I can. She will also tell you about how well I perform in class. She can give you all my reports if you need them. I am now in Grade Seven, my last year in primary school.

Before I go any further I want to apologise for calling you "you", as I tell our story. In our culture it's rude to call an adult "you", but Mistress Maluleke said I must call you like that as she thinks it's acceptable in your culture. Also, she does not know your name. She said she would write covering letters once she has found out all your names and made copies of this, our story, to send to as many businessmen as possible. That is the only chance we have of getting money to make our prayers and dreams come true. Everyone at LPS says it was Mistress Maluleke who wrote many letters to Papa Mandela asking him to build a school for us. She even travelled to Johannesburg to talk to Papa Mandela. When I asked her if that was true, she just smiled and said, "I just did my bit, child". The children want her to become the principal.

Now let me tell you about what Lesedi and I do each day. I wake up at 5am. I cook soft porridge for the two of us on the primus stove. I always make enough for breakfast and lunch if we have enough mieliemeal. While the porridge is cooking I go to clean our toilet. We still use pit toilets in our village, but ours is one of those nicer ones. Papa built a wooden seat so that we don't have to squat. It even has a lid that Papa made with his own hands many a Christmas holiday ago. Mme trained me to clean the toilet in the morning before it becomes too hot. The problem with too much heat is the flies and the smell. I don't mind the flies because I am used to them. It's the smell I can't stand. Now that we don't use wood for cooking, we don't have ash to throw down the toilet. The ash acts as air-freshener and it's just one of those things you cannot ask the neybars for because they use all theirs. It takes a lot of ash to take the smell away. Unlike salt that you only need to use a little at a time. The complicating thing is that I also cannot use a lot of soap. You see, soap also helps to deal with the smell, but even soap is becoming scarce. I save it.

Here is one area where Mistress Maluleke and I disagree. I will tell you about the others later. She said I must feel free to tell you my opinions as part of this story. She seems to think that I am not "as frugal as your mother was". I swear to you, my very name is frugal. She keeps telling me to live "parsimoniously". I always tell her, "Mistress, our very existence is parsimony."

Once the porridge is done, I wake Lesedi up and pray. Each night I pray that she doesn't pee in her bed. As I wake her up I also pray because there are days when she does it just before I wake her up. That is when I find that it's still hot and smells fresh. She sleeps on her own grass mat on the floor next to my bed. I make her sleep naked so that I have just one thing to wash because soap is such a problem. But I know that I cannot do that once winter comes. When Mme passed away, Lesedi went back to infancy.

This is where my first plea to you comes in. I have heard that there are tablets that Lesedi can take to help her stop urinating in her sleep. I am told they are very expensive. Your money will go a long way to help us with this. I would really like her to stop as it is affecting her. She starts talking to me rudely, you know, just plain disrespectful. I slap her when she speaks to me like that. Something happens to me, I know I should be patient with her.

If Lesedi's bed is wet, she takes forever to awaken. She turns and turns in her bed until I shout her name or slap her a little on the back. Once she is fully awake, I wash her face and private parts with very little water in a plastic bowl. I use the same water to wash her sheet.

I don't mind it so much when she wets herself over the weekend because that's when I do our washing. Mme said one should never ever leave soiled bed sheets unwashed: "It's unhygienic". She liked to use that word. Mme was a cleaner at the village clinic, so she knew all about it. She used to wash Papa's sheets and pyjamas every morning and as soon as he had messed on himself during the day. Luckily for me, Lesedi does not do the other thing in her sleep. Granny-next-door said I must not use napkins on Lesedi because that would be as good as giving her permission to wet herself. I think she has a good point. What do you think?

The porridge is usually cooked by the time I finish washing the sheet. I dish up the porridge, then put it aside to cool down. Once I finish the washing I wash my face and private parts quickly, just two hands full of water and a dash of soap. The problem comes with that time of the month. Blood is hard to wash out. It needs a lot of water and soap. Fortunately for me, I don't have to buy those expensive sanitary pads. I use the napkins that Mme used for Papa when he could not help himself. They were made from Lesedi's napkins that Mme sewed together to fit Papa. I cut them all up into small pieces and they work out fine. But they are not easy on the soap.

When we have eaten and dressed, I put Lesedi in our wheelbarrow and we go to school. We usually leave our house any time after 7am and definitely before 7.30am. Our school starts at 8.30am because many children come from very far away. It takes me just under an hour to reach school. I always leave Lesedi at Tsidi's home, which is just four homes away from school. I started doing this when Mme was still around because she and Tsidi's mother were very good friends. When Tsidi's mother also passed away, we agreed I could just continue doing this because Lesedi and Tsidi's baby sister have always been good friends.

Now allow me to take some time to tell you a side story about the wheelbarrow. Mme bought it from a farmer on the other side of the hill so that she could take Papa to the clinic once a week, as she did not have money for a taxi. Her salary went down to nothing after Papa came home because she started working only part-time at the clinic so she could be home to nurse Papa. She was attacked, verbally I mean, by many women for doing this. They called her a witch. They said it was undignified to put a man in a wheelbarrow, that she should be ashamed. Some said it would bring bad luck to our family.

This is one thing that Mme and Granny-next-door agreed on. She told Mme to just do what she thought was right and ignore the "stupid village women". And now I put Lesedi in the wheelbarrow, it makes my life so much easier. Granny-next-door gave me a big plastic that I put over Lesedi on rainy days. It's big enough to cover her completely. I use the same plastic between the grass mat and the sheet for Lesedi. That way I don't have to wash the grass mat. I used the wheelbarrow to take Lesedi to the clinic once when she was ill. On days when I don't feel like carrying the bucket of water on my head, I also use it. When I visited my uncle who lives two villages away, I used it. I will tell you about him later.

This brings me to my second prayer and my second disagreement with Mistress Maluleke. I pray every evening that a businessman will build a home for children, orphans who do not go to school and those who do not have homes. With that I would not have to feel bad about leaving Lesedi at Tsidi's home every day. Tsidi has two baby sisters. One is Lesedi's age and the other is only two. The younger one falls ill very often, and Tsidi has to miss school. Tsidi's father is a mining man just like Papa was, and he has never come home since their mother passed away. Fortunately for Tsidi he sends money every month.

Mistress Maluleke says, "There is money out there to give to AIDS orphans, the only question is how to access it." And I disagree. I think if there's money for AIDS orphans, there is money for orphans of any kind. That boy Mbuso is also looking after three siblings. Their parents were killed in a car accident when they went to a wedding in Johannesburg. Mbuso goes to high school in the next village and works after school and on weekends at Moosa's General Dealers. His brother and sisters are always at home alone until the store closes at seven. I whispered in his ears that Mistress Maluleke is making me write to you, that he should write as well. I mean, he is really a nice boy. Sometimes when I don't have enough money for soap, paraffin, candles and mieliemeal, he gives me some from his home. He once gave me margarine, such a luxury! Mr Moosa pays him in kind some times when he runs out of things for the house. So really I don't buy this "AIDS orphans" story that Mistress Maluleke calls "a fenomenon of our times".

Granny-next-door agrees with me on this. She was born in 1918 in the year when thousands of people died of influenza. She was lucky to have survived, with both her parents. She says she remembers that her own mother used to talk about how unfair it was that the whole community was more concerned about "influenza orphans" than other kinds of orphans. She says what is happening now with AIDS is just history repeating itself. And that history has to repeat itself because human beings take long to learn lessons about life. Granny-next-door speaks about a lot of things this way. I like listening to her though sometimes I think she speaks in confusing ways. Whenever I really miss Mme, I go to her to cry. Her sight is half gone so I don't mind crying in front of her. She tells me that nature has a way of dealing with things. She says this AIDS is here to "level things out", sometimes she calls it "creating a balance". She says all of us will become better adults for having experienced parenting as children.

When I arrive at Tsidi's, she finishes whatever she is doing and we walk to school together. It saddens me that she has to miss so many days when her baby sister is ill because she does not have brightness genes. Granny-next-door says the reason I do so well in school is because intelligence runs through my blood, my genes. After school I sit with Tsidi so we can do homework together before we go to face our sisters. It takes me a long time to get her to understand some of the things I help her with, particularly mathematics, science and English. Unfortunately our teachers are not as patient with those of us who are not so bright.

This is part of the reason I want to be the Minister of Education in my province one day. I really enjoy teaching less smart children at LPS. Do you know that I have already taught Lesedi to count up to twenty, yet she is just four? Granny-next-door says it's the intelligence genes doing that, not me. I hate it when she takes away my credit. It's a pity that when I am the Minister, she will be long gone. There are many things I will correct when I become the

Minister. Everyone, including Granny-next-door in her grave, will know that I did it.

Sorry, I went off a bit there. I have been writing this story for three days now. Tsidi wrote hers in one day, just one page, and gave it to Mistress Maluleke. I write a few pages before I start my homework. I then take it to the staffroom for safe-keeping in Mistress Maluleke's desk. She said I could write as long or as short a story as I liked, just as long as it is full of "pictures" for you to really understand our lives. Knowing Mistress Maluleke, I imagine that many children in other grades who also lost parents to this disease are also writing their stories. I have to go now. Till tomorrow, then.

"Mediocrity is the biggest problem black people impose upon themselves in this new South Africa. Women are better at it than men."

You guessed right, that's Mistress Maluleke speaking. She likes saying that. She said it again today in class during our Life Orientation period. When she says that, anger shines through her eyes and she punches the table and desks with her fists. But when she says that, I feel inspiration. I tell you this because she said I must explain in my story what keeps me going. I've never told her this, but each time I hear her say that, I begin to think positively. I don't want to be mediocre, ever.

When Papa passed away Mme went back to work at the clinic full-time. But a month later she was also ill. The head nurse at the clinic, Matron Sithole, said she would find a bed for Mme at the hospital because she knew the senior nurses there. She liked Mme very much. She said she was "a hard-working woman of little education". Mme first resisted going to hospital. Matron Sithole insisted. Granny-next-door persuaded Mme to accept Matron's offer by telling her that if her health worsened and I had to nurse her, I would have to miss school. That changed Mme's mind. So our routine changed. Every Friday afternoon, Matron sent Lesedi and I to visit Mme at the hospital. We went in the clinic ambulance. We would come back in the same ambulance on Saturday morning.

At the hospital they let us sleep there, Lesedi next to Mme and me with the "nursing mothers". These are women whose children are too small, so they are not allowed to go home until the children are big enough to survive outside of the, I think they call them intubators. How can I describe them to you? They are like little tents, made of glass so that each mother can watch her child growing. They have holes for the nurses and doctors put their hands through to touch the babies. Nurses and doctors never let me go near the intubators. I only saw them through the window.

Granny-next-door and some nurses said Mme was killed by exhaustion and a sore heart because really she was never as ill as Papa was. She could still walk to the toilet by herself, although she looked weak, and she played hand-touching games with Lesedi and told us stories right until the last day. Granny-next-door was sad that she never had a chance in those six weeks to visit Mme at the hospital.

Back to our daily routine, Tsidi doesn't like it very much when I help her with schoolwork during the homework period at school. On those days when I do not manage to persuade her to do homework at school, it's the first thing we do when we arrive at her home. When that is done we play with the children a bit, then I take Lesedi's wheelbarrow and we go home.

The first thing I do when we arrive home is work in the garden. Granny-next-door has a vegetable garden that she makes me work in for pay. I make R2.50 a week. Plus she says I can pick whatever I like. Her gardener is always picking enough to feed his family. For supper I cook stiff pap. In good times I mix it with something or put it on the side. Lesedi's favourite is potatoes mixed with pap. I prefer spinach. That day when Mbuso gave me margarine I added it, and as we say in our part of the world, "you couldn't give it to the blind".

Granny-next-door lives with her granddaughter who never did well at school and therefore works in town in white people's kitchens, and comes home every evening. Granny-next-door told me that all her five children still send her money at the end of each month. They send her so much money that she sometimes forgets to go and collect her pension money. She does not have many uses for money. That is why she sometimes gives me brown coins just for making her a cup of her own tea.

I am very anxious about winter coming. We are in the middle of April now. Winter has begun whispering to us.

When winter shouts there will be nothing in Granny-next-door's garden for us to have with pap.

I will tell you about our weekend when I write again next week. But to finish off our day, Lesedi and I eat supper together. After supper I teach Lesedi a few things, like today I want her to start counting from twenty backwards. After the lesson I read a bit to her, and then put her in bed. Candles are a big problem with us, on days when I am not as frugal as Mistress Maluleke says I must be, I use so much of the candle! I like to read. I take books from our school library every week. The problem is, there's just not enough time in the day to read. As you will have gathered by now, not one day goes by without me praying before I go to sleep. That's how I end my day.

I hope you had a good weekend. Ours was routine, as you will soon read. After Mme passed away, we used to go to the graveyard every Saturday morning. Lesedi used to talk to Mme for a long time, telling her stories and joking with her. That was one thing I could not stand, hearing her talk like that. It made me so sad I'd start crying. So I stopped going there. We went there this Saturday after a long time, just to clean it up. It was Granny-next-door's idea. I took a grass broom with me and picked up stones and wild flowers on the road. After I finished sweeping, I put the stones and flowers on both graves. Granny-next-door says I should always do this to show respect for my parents and all our ancestors. But she still will not tell me much about ancestors, just like Mistress Maluleke.

The weekend also means cleaning and tidying the house and yard thoroughly. We live in one hut. Our second house that was a proper mud house with two rooms went up in flames soon after Mme went to hospital. Remember I promised to tell you a story about my uncle? This is it. When he heard the news about Mme being in hospital, he came to our house to take all the furniture we had in the second house, even the stove that was in this hut. This hut served as a kitchen and the children's bedroom. The other house had Papa and Mme's bedroom and a living-room. On that day, Granny-next-door and other neybars saw him. He had two other men in the van helping him to move our things. He told them that Mme had given him permission to take everything because we would not need it. Then two weeks later, on a Saturday when we came back from the hospital, we found the second hut in ashes. No one saw anyone but the rumar in the village is that my uncle did it. I never told Mme about it. I made Lesedi swear that she would not tell. When I went to ask him to return some things we really needed, he told me that my family was shameful and he did not want to have anything to do with us. Now, as you know, many people have difficulties accepting this disease, but for me it was hard to discover that it was my family that had such problems. Most village people here have not given us any problems. Even at LPS, children and teachers talk about it as just a disease that we must find a cure for.

As I was saying, I clean the house inside and out. I wash our clothes. That means going to the communal water pump many times. I am usually done by about three in the afternoon. Lesedi often helps here and there. We spend the rest of the afternoon looking for food: fruits, nuts and edible greens that grow in the wild. We also catch edible insects. Almost all the village children do this on Saturday afternoons. Lesedi just loves it. It's not just fun (we play lots of games in the process); it also means that we don't depend on Granny-next-door for vegetables. Mme always said we should live within our means. There was one Saturday when we found so much food we did not need any vegetables from the garden next door. That Saturday I asked Granny-next-door if we could use her paraffin fridge to keep our greens.

On Sunday mornings we go to Sunday school at LPS. This is when I consolidate all my prayers. My biggest prayer of them all is to fulfil Mme's dream. Before Papa passed away, Mme was trying to get his pension money from the mine where he worked. Every Saturday she sent me to Moosa's General Dealers to check if an envelope had come for her. It never came. Mme's problem was that she did not know the name of the mine where Papa worked. She did not know how to follow up. Even Mrs Sithole (the matron at her clinic) said it would be hard to trace the money if Mme did not have the name of the mine. This is where we need your help. Can you please help trace Papa's mine and employer. The information I have on him is the following:

Name: Brian (Boetie) Vukani Lekalakala
Profession: Coal Miner (Digger)

Name of mine: ? in Johannesburg

Date of starting work: been there since a young man of approximately 25 years

Home village: Bhekilanga Village in Limpopo province

I am still keeping Papa's ID book, as I had to take it with me every Saturday to Moosa's General Dealers when Mme sent me to look for Papa's pension money. I still use it for the same reason, therefore I cannot give it you now. I imagine you will need it for tracing purposes. Just let me know.

If we can get this money, most of our problems will be solved. The money Mme left in her post office account (she did not have a bank account) was only R150. Our post office is a mobile one. It comes to our clinic once a month on the first Friday of the month. With Matron Sithole helping, the post office people allowed me to change the name of the account holder even though I am a minor. She told them I was a "responsible and smart orphaned child-parent". I have been using this money for groceries, and there's now only R25 left. My genes help with my school fees. Mistress Maluleke said I would have no problem getting a bursary for high school and university. But we need the money for our living expenses (mainly food, many candles, paraffin, lots of soap and clothes) and for Lesedi when she starts school. For now she seems to be a bright child, but if we don't get her to stop wetting her bed at night, she might change. I've heard people say bedwetting makes you dull. It affects your head somehow. That would mean she couldn't get bursaries for her education.

I hope that you now have the full picture of our lives. Let me end by emfasising that I am asking that you help us with the three things I mentioned above. If you help us with those, my sister and I will be fully on our own in no time. I therefore appeal to your good heart, your kind spirit and sensibilities, to answer my prayers.

Inside

HER STEPMOTHER'S VOICE rings through her head: "Always take something – anything. It's rude not to. Even the smallest thing will do." Bhekiwe parks her car and walks toward Killarney Mall. It's just after nine in the morning. She remembers seeing a flower shop close to the entrance. Flowers. That should do.

She finds the florist right where she thought it would be. Amid mounds of flowers she sees five small pots of pale pink miniature roses. She is drawn to them. She likes the size, just right for a first visit to someone's home. But she doesn't like the formal look of the arrangement. Also, they are roses. But there is nothing else miniature.

She veers towards the bunches of wild-looking, multi-coloured chrysanthemums. She recalls reading in a magazine that Chinese gardeners were the first to cultivate this flower from indigenous perennials. They wrote many songs and poems about it. And Confucius was the first to record the presence of this flower as far back as 500 BC. She'd read this just three days ago, in a hair salon. She likes their multiple colours, but the flowers are a bit too loud – and too large for a first visit.

Her eyes skim over numerous arrangements in silver pots to one containing single strelitzias. They are called birds of paradise – she recalls reading this somewhere, too. These are just right. The shape of the petals suggests both pride and humility. The colours are a surprisingly fitting mix. She picks three stems. Three is a fine number for a first visit. She pays. The cashier assures her that she has made a good choice. She heads out of the mall building.

Zodwa had told her that the Seven Palms block of flats was on the road leading from the mall parking lot. She told her to keep walking – no turns, keep looking right – it wouldn't be too far to walk. As she walks, her mind returns to the day she first noticed Zodwa, almost a year ago.

It was at a parents' meeting at Holy Mary College. Bhekiwe was attending the meeting at her father's request, as he had a business meeting to attend. She watched, listened and took notes. Each time the discussion strayed, Zodwa stood up to remind the meeting what the focus of the discussion was. She used her hands a lot when she spoke. Bhekiwe admired Zodwa's fingers. Slim, very slim, as if trimmed to look just right. She wondered what cream Zodwa used on her hands.

Zodwa was the teacher representative on the School Governing Body, and so she was at each of the subsequent meetings that Bhekiwe attended on those occasions her father couldn't make it.

One day, Bhekiwe asked her one brother if he knew the name of the teacher who always wore loose pants, loose tops and colourful head wraps.

"Miss Black."

"Is that what you call her – why?"

"She was always in black, like, always. Well, in that first month when she came to our school."

"Really?"

"Now she wears other colours, not many, but the name kinda, like, stuck."

"Is she a good teacher?"

'She doesn't teach me, but my friend says she's, like, very strict. He hates her.'

"What subjects does she teach?"

"Physical Education and isiZulu, juniors only. Why do you care, Sis'Bheks?"

For a moment Bhekiwe was silent, asking herself the same question.

"Curious. I'm just curious. Anything wrong with that?" She realised she was speaking to the wind. Her brother was already running towards the car.

On prize-giving day, Bhekiwe made a point of sitting next to Zodwa.

"Hi there. Anyone sitting here, Ms Black?"

"Oh, hi there, Ms Beautiful."

It was the first time someone apart from her father had called her beautiful without it sounding like an insult. Who would ever have thought being beautiful could be such a curse?

"My name is Ntombizodwa. Non-learners call me Zodwa for short. What's your name?"

Their hips and thighs touched. Bhekiwe noticed how firm Ms Black's hips were. Much firmer than hers. She wanted to remark on it, but quickly commanded the idea to go away. In fact, her stepmother's voice uttered the caution: "Bhekiwe, that would be rude."

When the event was over, they wished each other season's greetings, and did not see each other to speak to again until the following year.

A month after school reopened, Bhekiwe was waiting for her brothers near the main gate when Zodwa walked past. Bhekiwe stepped out of the car and greeted her. They exchanged a few words. Zodwa surprised her by asking if she would join a group of her friends at Kippies Jazz Club.

"We all love Taiwa, come join us. It's a women's night out."

Bhekiwe had no idea who Taiwa was, but she agreed. The only jazz artists she knew were her father's favourites, whom she had begun to like via osmosis.

During the show, Zodwa asked why she was named Bhekiwe.

"I thought you teach isiZulu, don't you know what Bhekiwe means?"

"Of course I do – I'm asking why *you* were given that name."

Bhekiwe was embarrassed to realise that she had never asked her father. During a break, she rang her father, and then told Zodwa the story: because she was born in exile, there was no family around to help raise her. This had made her father anxious. He named her Bhekiwe to reflect his wish that their relatives and the spirits of the ancestors would look after her.

That evening, Zodwa talked a lot to her other friends and colleagues. As her hands moved, Bhekiwe noticed a thin copper bangle embracing her left wrist. When Zodwa's hand moved closer to hers, Bhekiwe caught a whiff of citrus fruit and wondered again what hand cream Zodwa used. She made a mental note to ask her, on another day, at another moment. At the end of the show, Zodwa went home with a colleague. Bhekiwe did not see her again for a couple of months.

Then, the day before school closed for the winter holidays, Bhekiwe was helping out by fetching her brothers from school. She offered Zodwa a lift home. When they arrived at Killarney, Zodwa suggested they have coffee before she went off to buy groceries. Bhekiwe's brothers went to the bookshop while she and Zodwa talked, sharing stories about their families.

Bhekiwe confided, "Daddy has been unlucky – his fiancée died a few months before they got married. My mother died two years after I was born, and my stepmother a year after my baby brother was born."

"Ag shame man, Bheks, that's too much for your old man."

"I know, I know. He says he'll never get married again."

"What was your father's fiancée's name?"

Zodwa's question surprised Bhekiwe – she'd never asked. But this time, instead of calling her father, she asked why Zodwa wanted to know.

"The short answer is, I'm curious. The long answer is, I care."

"Care, care about what?"

"History."

Zodwa then went on to tell Bhekiwe she was the last of five children, two of whom had died of AIDS, and one in a car accident. Zodwa paid school fees for two nieces and a nephew, all in schools in Limpopo. She also supported her mother, who lived with the three grandchildren. She'd come to Johannesburg when she got the position as a physical education teacher – her passion. In Limpopo, no school would employ her; they said they preferred male teachers because they were better at sport.

Then she smiled, changing the subject: "Hey listen, Bheks, enough of this family stuff. Would you like go to a poetry session with me one of these days?"

"Didn't know you're a poet."

"I'm not, I just write a poem or two now and again. But I love listening to poets do their thing."

"Will you let me read some of your poems, then?"

Zodwa announced that she needed to buy a few groceries before Pick 'n Pay closed. She stood up, grabbed her handbag, took out a notebook and said, "I bought this notebook last week, there are two poems in there that you can read. Tell me what you think."

Then Zodwa waved goodbye and half-ran out of the coffee shop.

A rather bemused Bhekiwe got up and found her brothers engrossed in their books in the deep couches at Exclusive Books next door.

It has been a quick walk to the Seven Palms, and Bhekiwe is filled with anticipation. With the strelitzias in one hand and Zodwa's notebook in her bag, she rings the bell. After greeting the security guard at the desk, commenting on the weather and signing the register, she asks if Zodwa is in. He tells her that Zodwa has just got back from her morning run. When the lift reaches the third floor, Bhekiwe steps out, turns left, presses the buzzer at number 34 while calling Zodwa's name, and waits. The door opens. Zodwa stands there, her hair hanging free and shiny black. Her tightly twisted locks fall with abandon over her collar bones. She is in her running gear: a pair of long black stretch pants and a black athletic top. The gap between the top and pants reveals tight abdominal muscles, with a soft line of hair running down from the navel. Bhekiwe wonders what it would feel like under her fingers.

They stand silent for a split second.

Bhekiwe has never imagined Zodwa in close-fitting clothes, despite knowing that she teaches physical education. What she now sees is what her aunt would call "a sculpture of womanhood". Her aunt used to say that the reason some women had such artistic bodies is because women made their own moulds when God took a break. What Bhekiwe really wants to ask is why Zodwa always wears baggy pants and loose tops that hang over her hips, hiding this sculpture "I remembered it's the first day of school holidays. I thought you might be home. Sorry, I should have called. Your notebook."

She holds out the flowers and the notebook, and her handbag slides down her shoulder to just below her elbow. Zodwa repositions Bhekiwe's handbag, touching her arm as she does so. Bhekiwe looks down at her arm as if it is not a part of her body. Then, as if in slow motion, Zodwa moves her hand away, saying that the flowers are beautiful.

"No need to apologise. I'm glad you're here. Come in. How're things?"

"Fine, fine, in fact better than fine. I decided I'm sick and tired of being exhausted. I'm taking three days off. Boss lady agreed. And guess what? I'm not even going to be working on my Masters. My supervisor is off to a conference in Kampala."

"Coffee?"

Zodwa leads the way to the kitchen. Bhekiwe notices the muscles on Zodwa's shoulders and upper arms. The JT top she is wearing seems designed to show off such firm shoulders. The shine of sweat reminds her of massage oil. With a quick shake of the head, she forces herself to focus on the moment. She notices the lounge area, which is almost bare of furniture. There are two tall bookshelves along one wall, cushions scattered on the carpet, and in a corner, a music system and a stand stacked with compact discs – over a hundred, Bhekiwe estimates.

"I liked your poems, Zodwa. They're beautiful."

"You have to say more than that. What exactly did you like?"

"The simplicity, the truth. And I feel as if I've learnt more about you."

"Really? You'll have to tell me more about that."

The kitchen is narrow. It's a glorified corridor. Bhekiwe settles on the breakfast stool, wriggling her bottom as if that will create more space. Zodwa busies herself with mugs, coffee beans, the French press, milk and sugar.

"How's the research going?"

Bhekiwe's research focuses on women who are organised into small craft groups – in her case, beadwork – how they survive economically, and how labour laws affect them.

"Have you narrowed down your research area yet? The last time we spoke, that was your plan."

"Ja, well, we're getting there. My supervisor agrees with you. She says I must just focus on the women, since that's what I'm most interested in – interview them, you know, in-depth personal interviews, and forget about labour laws and the economics of it all."

"Mm … but it sounds like you're still married to your old idea?"

Bhekiwe takes a packet of Cartier Menthols and a lighter from her brown handbag. "Can I step onto the balcony, please?" She opens the back door, and after closing it again slightly, she lights a cigarette.

Half-shouting, Zodwa asks, "Does your father know you haven't stopped?"

"Zo, let's not go there. Daddy knows I'm stressed right now."

"So Daddy lets his Bheks smoke herself to her grave?"

Bhekiwe shuts the door with a bang. Didn't Zodwa remember what she'd told her about her father's repeated encounters with death? After a while, she opens the door again and returns to her seat in the kitchen.

"Sorry, Bheks, I didn't mean it that way."

"Sure, no sweat. Where were we?"

"Your women bead-jewellery makers, their life stories versus their economic survival and problems with labour laws."

"Ja, well, for my sanity I think I'll stick to personal histories. It makes more sense. And it's simpler."

"Talking of personal histories – I need to shower, my period is on. You don't mind waiting, right? Go listen to some music in the lounge. We'll carry on talking about your research afterwards while I make us breakfast."

"Zo, what has your period got to do with personal histories?"

"Well, let's see, I started menstruating the day before my fifteenth birthday. I'm thirty-two years old. That's seventeen years; 204 months of bleeding. But I missed six months when I was 19 because of medication I was on. In 1985, I was in prison during the State of Emergency, and my period disappeared. Stress, I think, but it was only for three months. I've been regular since. That brings the total down to 195 months. Can you imagine how many litres of blood that is?"

Zodwa stands up, smiles with her head slanted to the left, and disappears into the bathroom.

Bhekiwe drinks her coffee and ponders. The talk of menstrual blood has awakened her vagina. She feels a sudden seeping of juices, and smiles to herself.

Minutes later, she walks to the lounge. She reaches for Taiwa's *Genes and Spirits*, and the lounge absorbs the vibrations. She chooses the largest cushion and sits on it, supporting the small of her back with a smaller navy-blue one. She wants to know who Zodwa really is, but she doesn't even know what questions to ask. All she knows for sure is that Zodwa is unlike any of her four close friends. They are all the children of returnees – and she's only known one of them since childhood. She met the others through their parents, who hold regular get-togethers to talk about the struggle, their countries of exile, the democratic government – its foibles and fortunes, black economic empowerment deals, and affirmative action.

She wants to page through the books on the shelves. Her stepmother would say it was rude to go through someone's bookshelf without permission, but she doesn't feel like shouting a request in the direction of the bathroom.

Just sitting like that, with Taiwa in the background, is enough for the moment. Her mind goes back to that night at Kippies: the copper bangle on a narrow but strong wrist; the whiff of citrus fruit in the jazzy night air of Jozi; firm thighs under a pair of black pants. She sees Taiwa's soft elongated face, his moustache and beard that needed trimming, his far-seeing eyes, his half-smile, and his nimble fingers on the keyboard. When the track "Genes and Spirits" plays, it transports her to the dusty streets of her childhood in Tanzania. There's a sound to it, a cadence that she recognises as belonging somewhere north of here. She feels the humid Tanzanian air embrace her body, caressing her skin, easing into her pores. She closes her eyes and wonders why this track had not produced the same feeling that night at Kippies. But then Taiwa's rhythms change, evoking other places.

"'Spirits of Tembisa', it's my favourite track on that CD."

Bhekiwe looks up at Zodwa, who is now wearing a pair of loose-fitting black tracksuit pants. The long-sleeved jacket is fully zipped up in front. She is back to being the real Ms Black. A black head-wrap covers her twisted hair. She has a look of preparedness.

"Are you dreaming, Bheks? I'm not surprised. Taiwa has this knack of taking you away, somewhere far, where you've never been."

Slowly Bhekiwe gets up from the floor: "Oh, sorry – you were saying?"

"I was saying I'd like to find a place inside you, that I'd take somewhere you've never been."

"And where is that?"

But Zodwa turns away, showing Bhekiwe her back.

"To the kitchen. Come, I'll make us breakfast. Follow me."

Zodwa walks to the kitchen, Bhekiwe behind her. Bhekiwe's eyes are fixed on the head-wrap, and she visualises Zodwa's hair hanging against her bare shoulders, as it had just a few minutes ago. She peeps into the bedroom as they walk past. A black and white bed cover dominates the room.

As they step into the kitchen, Bhekiwe prompts, "You were saying something else…"

"Nothing much, I was just saying I love that track, 'Spirits of Tembisa'. You know, after listening to it a few times, I decided to go to Tembisa."

"Oh, really? Is it *that* good?"

"Dunno, there's something about those drums, Bheks, you can only understand it once you've been to the place. Funnily enough, I love it for the drums rather than the piano."

"Hmm, I must listen to it again."

"And then go to Tembisa?"

They laugh.

As Zodwa starts to prepare breakfast, Bhekiwe asks, "What's your other favourite track, then?"

"'Finding oneself'. It's on his other CD of the same title."

"Where did you take off to after listening to that one?"

"My core."

"Your core?"

"Yes, my core; you know, inside me – where it all begins."

Silence.

Bhekiwe looks around the kitchen as if in search of something. The yellow cabinets and black floor tiles do not give her an answer. She suddenly feels uncomfortable on the bar stool. The padding is too thin. The circumference is not wide enough. Her elbows are not in a relaxed position. She remembers how she had discouraged her father and brothers from buying bar stools for their kitchen. This was three years ago when they'd bought furniture for their new home in Rivonia. Her brothers teased her about her "massive behind", but her father had supported her. The vote was split, so the adults won.

Bhekiwe climbs down and goes out onto the balcony without another word. When she's finished smoking, Zodwa starts, "Back to your research. What stage are you at now?"

"Forget about my research for now. I asked Daddy about his fiancée's name."

Zodwa's face opens up. Her dimples deepen. Her eyebrows lift toward her hairline. Even her earlobes seem to curl forwards.

"And?"

Bhekiwe is surprised by an urgent desire to dip the tip of her index finger into Zodwa's dimple. She feels embarrassment deep inside her stomach and rearranges her face to suppress the feeling.

"You're not going to believe it," she smiles.

"Hey, I haven't seen that kind of smile on your face before! It's not a smile, actually. What is it?"

"Zo, have you been monitoring my smiles?"

"Bheks, I teach a language. But people don't only speak with words, they speak with their faces and their bodies, too. My job is to watch."

"I see. Well, you have the most athletic body I have ever seen."

Again, there is a split second of silence.

"Don't change the subject. What was her name?"

"Bhekiwe."

"Seriously, Bheks? Her name was Bhekiwe? Now isn't that something! Do you think your mother knew?"

"I have no idea, Zo. Daddy doesn't like talking about the three women who, as he puts it, 'died in his hands'."

Zodwa was quiet for a while, then asked, "How do you like your egg?"

"Sunny side up."

"So, Bheks, what's the next question you're asking Daddy?"

"No, Zo, my father can only deal with one question at a time. Same with me – with this, at least. It all feels a bit eerie."

"Sure. I can imagine. Your father loves you, Bheks."

"Can we talk about something else, please?"

The oil in the pan releases a whiff of smoke. Zodwa moves it off the hot plate and reaches for the eggs from the fridge. Before she fries the eggs, she puts two slices of brown bread in the toaster. Bhekiwe's hand reaches for it.

"No, no, no, you are the visitor here, don't," Zodwa pulls the toaster away from Bhekiwe until it almost disconnects from the power point. They laugh.

Zodwa takes two tomatoes from a vegetable basket made of tightly woven grass, cuts each into quarters, then puts them on the plates, next to the toast and eggs. Bhekiwe is relieved when Zodwa does not suggest that they say grace – as her brothers always insist she should.

For a while they eat in silence. Sunrays pour over Zodwa's right shoulder and onto their plates. It's warming up. The morning cloud and the weather report had suggested a much cooler day. Bhekiwe feels a tinge of excitement at the idea of a warm winter day. However, the weather is the last thing she wants to talk about.

"So, how do you like Holy Mary College?"

"I love my job. But I'm not so sure about the school."

"Why?"

"Catholicism and education: deadly combination. I would think thrice before sending my child there."

Bhekiwe makes a note to herself to ask her brother about this apparently lethal combination. Zodwa seems to expect that she knows something about Catholicism when in fact she doesn't have a dot of an idea. She thinks about her father, who decided that Holy Mary College would be the perfect school for her brothers because Mandela's grandchildren went there. She makes another mental note to ask her father if he'd done any of his own research on the school, and what he knows about the Catholic faith. She wants to ask Zodwa more, but the right question does not come.

"You run a lot, don't you? Do you do races?"

"Yes, as many as I can. This evening I'll do a short, fast run. I'm training for a marathon."

"And in between?"

"What could be better than reading? I read all day long."

They eat in silence. Bhekiwe's mind drifts. Her gaze shifts. She lifts her eyes from her plate to Zodwa's chest, wondering what she is wearing under her jacket. She eats mechanically. Then her meandering mind finds a warm, welcoming and self-affirming space. She goes inside. Deeper.

When they finish eating, Zodwa boils the kettle again and serves coffee.

"I must go. It's going on for eleven already. Thanks for breakfast and coffee and everything."

They get up at the same time. Bhekiwe collects her bag, stretches slightly, and walks towards the door. A thought enters her mind – she's got to get going with that weight-loss programme she's been postponing. Zodwa is three years older than her, but she looks five years younger. When she reaches the door, Bhekiwe steps aside to let Zodwa open it and let her through.

They bid each other farewell. As Bhekiwe walks to the lift three doors away, Zodwa waits at the door. Bhekiwe feels her eyes between her shoulder blades. At the lift, she turns around to discover that these eyes are accompanied by a smile, one she cannot explain. She waves goodbye.

Before Bhekiwe turns on the car engine, she opens her diary to make a list of things to do. "Finding oneself', she writes – but nothing more. She tries to remember the mental notes she'd made earlier that day. Nothing. Then she starts up the engine. And as she drives out of the parking bay, pays, and continues into an unplanned day, she can feel Zodwa's smiling eyes lingering on her.

The Trip

QHAMUKILE WONDERED WHY people spoke of feelings as being in the chest. Having thought of them that way for a long time made her feel them, right there, in her chest. The fullness was unbearable.

She spent time telling her chest to relax, but it would not. Then she decided to focus on the road, or rather on things around the road. She had been focusing on the road for at least an hour now.

The journey began that morning at about five. The alarm clock went off one second after she opened her eyes and wondered whether it was time to wake up yet. She left the bed and went straight to the toilet, then to the kitchen to turn on the kettle. When the water boiled she made a cup of tea, then walked back to her bedroom to enjoy it in bed. This was the best way to enjoy one's first morning cup. That done, she packed their picnic bag. She hated buying food from roadside stores. Her daughter's favourite foods all went in: Oros, a cheese sandwich, a banana, Tinkies and chocolate muffins that she had baked the previous night. For herself, she packed apples, fresh juice and peanuts. A friend had told her it was important to pack foods that would keep you awake as you drove, keep you chewing hard. Peanuts and apples it was going to be. After all, on your first five-hour drive you have to take your absolute favourites.

She had made plenty of muffins so she could take umngenandlini as well, even though baking had taken so long that she had only gone to bed at midnight. The chocolate muffins were for her daughter, the bran for her mama, and the banana for her mama's neighbour, MaMkhize. Qhamukile was not going to go to her mama's house without bringing MaMkhize muffins. MaMkhize had long declared her love for fresh-baked muffins.

Her mama had known MaMkhize for fifteen years. She was there when Mama moved to the area. She took care of Mama's orientation. She did more than invite her for meals at home with other women. She informed Mama about deaths and funerals in the neighbourhood, and made sure Mama attended. She explained relationships among the neighbours, infusing life to their characters. MaMkhize also listed the names of men whose wives had died, explaining the circumstances surrounding their death. MaMkhize's husband had left her for a younger woman. She had four daughters who had each had a child without getting married to the father. She was now raising the four grandchildren while her two younger daughters were finishing higher education. Qhamukile was looking forward to current news about the neighbourhood. She was sure MaMkhize would make time to tell her everything.

Bathing was going to take too long, so Qhamukile decided to do a wipe. It involved a few strokes: face, armpits, between the legs. For the first round she used soap, none for the second. For the third round, a dry towel sufficed. I must start taking care of my face, she thought.

Another friend had told her that as a woman approaching forty, she must start looking after her face, proper cleansing, no soap, toner (whatever that was) and moisturiser. It's very simple, her friend had explained. Once in the morning and once in the evening, and you get used to it. She could not see where she could fit such a rigorous routine in her schedule. So she kept postponing. There must be some truth in it though, because this friend had a face like a child's, and she claimed she had been using these things since her late teens. She laughed as she recalled her friend's voice: "Friend, it's an investment."

Putting clothes on was the quickest, three pairs of things, a panty and a bra, tracksuit top and bottom, socks and running shoes.

The next steps were the most irritating ones; taking all the sets of keys to open the front gate, the front door, the side gate and the side door, the garage gate and the car door, six keys in all! She returned to the house to fetch three bags: two suitcases (hers and her daughter's) and the picnic bag. These were waiting next to the front door, in her usual style of needing no hassle in the morning. When all was packed into the car, she locked it and went back to get her daughter from her bed. They had agreed she would be transplanted from her own bed to the back seat of the car. The blankets were waiting in position on the seat.

Helping her daughter Nontshisekelo out of bed also meant carrying her to the toilet, and while supporting her torso, encouraging her to release her bladder with characteristic motherly sounds. Nontshisekelo was able to urinate with her eyes completely closed. Simultaneously, she mastered a certain limpness that only a mother could understand, at this hour, during this activity. No amount of friendly advice could help Qhamukile with this part. Her daughter had not come with a recipe book.

The petrol tank had been filled the evening before, the tyres checked, water, oil, even the spare tyre. All her friends were concerned about her first long drive. They each had a piece of advice for her. They all agreed this was a major step in her life. Her first car, her first daughter, her first long ride.

At exactly six o'clock she inserted the ignition key, put the car in reverse, made sure the lights and the seat belts were on, and she was out of her driveway, clockwork perfect. She felt like shouting "hooray".

She tried turning the radio on, but could not tune it properly. The hiss was too irritating. After turning it off, she had her thoughts and the road to work with. Occasionally she quickly turned to look at her daughter. Each time Qhamukile managed to steal a look, her daughter seemed to have timed her smile just for her. When she noticed the same thing for the fourth time, she decided to pull over. It was true, her girl was having a long lovely dream, she could not stop smiling. She kissed her daughter lightly and returned to driving.

Driving in southeast from Johannesburg was like a free show of natural beauty. At this hour the horizon was doing its thing, with colours in the sky changing to announce the rising sun. The clouds and the sky seemed to have rehearsed this gracious performance. She thought of singers announcing the arrival of the bride, the joy, the voices. The skies and clouds seemed to understand this well. The colours were the mystery. The kind of mystery it's best not to unravel.

She watched, took it in. Her thoughts danced between the beauty in front of her, her daughter, her mama and herself.

She was the happiest woman today. The further she travelled from the skyscrapers she could see in her rear-view mirror, the more exhilarated she became. She recalled the day she first arrived in Johannesburg, on a long-distance bus, seven months pregnant, no home, a new and sort-of first job, and no bank account. A rural girl who had won a few battles and was prepared to win a few more. But she had never been pregnant before, had never felt so alone, never been to Johannesburg and never been thirty-four years old. Those days were fading from her memory.

The drama that had transformed her free-woman status to that of single parent was now filling her memory bank. She turned once again to look at her daughter, whose face was now turned away. She wondered whether another expression had replaced the smile.

Her mama would be surprised, as she always was. "Awakhula ntombazana!" she would say, clapping her hands and simultaneously planting a kiss on her forehead. Qhamukile loved this, watching her own mama as a grandparent. Although there were thirteen other grandchildren from her siblings, she had never had the chance to watch the relationship her mama had with her grandchildren so closely. This made it different, entertaining and very special. She even enjoyed calling her own mama "Gogo", just as all the grandchildren did. She knew Mama would have bought something as a surprise gift for her grand-daughter. She always managed to come up with a surprise each time they were together, or on her daughter's birthdays.

The first birthday present for her daughter had been a dress that Mama had made, one of those dresses that could be worn on either side. It would have won first prize in any competition. She had kept this dress after giving away lots of other clothes to the many friends who had had children after her.

She started picturing their dinner. Gogo insisted on well-balanced meals. She grew vegetables in her small garden: spinach, carrots, butternut, potatoes and amadumbe. "Qham'qham," she could hear her mama say, "your favourite, amadumbe, will you have them for starters or for dessert?" Qhamukile loved amadumbe so much that she insisted they should be enjoyed unadulterated. The Gauteng soil had no experience with this rare vegetable, so she really missed the exotic taste. She made up her mind to have them for starters tonight. She was planning to arrive at her mama's house at about 11am. Mama had this habit of preparing a range of treats as welcome-home eats. Dinner had to be nutritious and balanced, but the welcoming goodies were, in fact, junk food. Mama's theory was that the body replenishes itself during sleep and needs good food to do that just before bedtime.

The sun was fully out, a very deep red. Qhamukile put on her sunglasses. They added a veneer of majesty to the deep red finery. She wished her daughter were awake so she could also witness this free display of splendour.

As a child, Qhamukile had imagined that the act of dying involved disappearing into something. The idea of disappearing into the core of this sun was blissful. It's a pity the sun was so hot. If death were as simple as choosing an object to disappear into, purple clouds like these would be grand. The colour you see just after heavy summer rains, during sunset. That would be disappearing into magnificence.

The first tollgate sign appeared. Damn, she hated tollgates. She was glad she had remembered to put all her loose change into the car ashtray they used as a moneybox. This way she did not have to fish her handbag from between her feet. She had been pleased in the past when the taxi-drivers had to pay. But she was relieved that the taxi rides were a thing of the past. Years and years of long-distance taxi rides of up to six hours each was enough to drive anyone to self-mutilation.

Slowing down to pay at the Wilgeplaza tollgate made her realise just how exhausted she was. She was relieved to slow down. She noticed she was drowsy as well. Harrismith wasn't far away, and then she would stop, take a break, have a cup of coffee and let her daughter play. It's better to stop at places where other drivers stop. You even meet interesting people, one of her friends had declared knowingly.

Nontshisekelo had opened her eyes when the car slowed down, but was too drowsy to respond when Qhamukile tried talking to her. She let her be. She had to find something to actively occupy her mind. Driving was making her weary. The radio reception was fading in and out, so she turned it off. The hills and mountains on each side of the road were making things difficult for this technology.

She started to sing aloud, songs from childhood, whatever came first. Then she went through poems from primary school. Then she sang the nursery rhymes that her daughter loved so much, one after the other. Then she noticed that many cars were stopping ahead – an accident maybe? As she drew closer, she realised that the traffic police had stopped many taxis and two private cars. Three traffic police cars were interspersed between the taxis and cars.

Seven taxis were lined up next to the road, with their passengers all out of the vehicles, stretching their legs, walking briskly, eating, drinking and talking. Some children, with their mothers' help, were squatting to relieve themselves next to the road, some men were doing so as well, and others directed their fluid under the taxis they were riding.

She felt her heart miss a beat, then wondered what that was about, because she was as legal as could be; a new faultless, licensed car, her driver's license, seat belts on –

including her daughter's, even though it had been hard to put it around her horizontal body – no alcohol, no dagga. The dagga in her house was stashed very far away. It had never come anywhere close to her car, because she always insisted that her friend Rita had to come to her house if she wanted to enjoy it. Rita must really stop this habit, over the past few months she had been visiting more frequently. At least her friend was aware of her tendency to overindulge, enough to want to ask for help. But the problem with Rita was that she did not talk. As friends, they were all painfully aware of just how happy she was, always joking, insisting on fun, fun and more fun, but never a word about her personal life.

The traffic police did not stop her. With clipboards in their hands as they wrote and spoke to the drivers, they were earning their salary.

"Are we there yet?"

"No baby, we are not even halfway there yet."

"How long will it be before we stop? I'm hungry."

"About half an hour, baby. Why don't you try sleeping again? I'll wake you up when we arrive."

Her daughter threw the blanket aside but did not sit up.

"Do you think Gogo is up now waiting for us?"

"No, baby, it's too early for Gogo to wake up."

She sat up.

"Did I miss sunrise, Mama? Why didn't you wake me up? You promised to."

"I tried baby, I tried, but you were just too sleepy. You didn't say a word when I called your name."

"See, you never do what I say you must do, you didn't try hard enough. If you had, I would have seen the sun waking us up. This belt is irritating me."

"Nontshi, don't you start now, you know the rules."

She curled up again, pulling the blanket over her whole body and face.

"Promise you'll wake me up at the halfway stop."

"I promise."

"Promise, promise, promise."

Qhamukile yawned, her thighs heavy, her feet stiff. She pressed harder on the accelerator, the speedometer rose to 140. Twenty more kilometres and they would be in Harrismith.

The sign announcing Montrose planted a smile on Qhamukile's face. After she indicated, turned and stopped next to the only petrol pump that was free, she called her daughter's name.

Nontshisekelo responded with, "Are we there, are we there?"

If it weren't for the child lock, she would have seen herself out the car in one swift movement. Qhamukile talked to Nontshisekelo, responding to her questions while talking to the petrol attendant. Yes, he could check the water and the oil and yes, the front window needed cleaning, thank you very kindly.

The halfway stop was abuzz. Besides cars and taxis, three long distance buses were also parked: Greyhound, Translux and City to City. The parking bays were almost full. Qhamukile remembered the relief she had always felt when the bus or taxi stopped at these places. She was always surprised at how fresh the air smelled once they alighted. People milled around the restaurants, the coffee shop, the gift and craft shop, the grocery store; and the queues in the toilets were long.

With Nontshisekelo's hand in hers, Qhamukile stood in the queue to the toilets. Nontshisekelo was leading the conversation about what Gogo might be doing at this very moment, what they would eat, whether she could play on the swings at this stop, like her mother had promised, what Qhamukile had seen while she was asleep, whether she could have sweets after their meal, and how long it would take to arrive at Gogo's home.

They walked back to the car to take out their food so they could enjoy the "halfway picnic", as Nontshisekelo had taken to calling it. But first Nontshisekelo wanted to play on the swing, then go up and down the slide a few times while her mother watched. Another family with two children came to join them. The younger boy was the same height as Nontshisekelo. The two hit it off, laughing and giggling, and soon they were running around the stretch of green grass, their families seemingly forgotten.

Qhamukile found a shady spot between the willow trees and a pond full of white lilies. She sat down and began to eat. Her eyes darted from her meal to her daughter in that learnt parental guardedness. No doubt about it, Nontshisekelo was a happy four-year old.

The racially mixed couple kissed, clinging to each other, and laughing in between kisses. Qhamukile wondered how long they had been married, if they were married at all. What was it like to be married? Money, they must have enough money, with joint salaries. Her own financial situation was perpetually dicey. She had not plucked up enough fury to face her daughter's father about maintenance. Marriage must be such a serious commitment, though; so many things to disagree over and consult about. Then there were the families on either side. All her siblings were married, and the family meetings upon meetings that Qhamukile had witnessed over the years made her think it was just fine to be on her own. But this couple looked genuinely happy together. Maybe this was the answer for the future: inter-racial marriages. They produced beautiful children with striking features, and they were more amenable to openness. When people started off knowing they were so different, they were more likely to strive towards convergence, better understanding, unity and general openness about relationships and life. And the children could then be raised with the best of both worlds.

The older boy, who could be anything between eleven and thirteen years old, had his father's black curly hair, while the younger boy's hair was less curly and as brown as his mother's. The older boy sat on the grass with a Walkman and earphones in his ears. The two boys were decidedly handsome.

When she lifted her eyes from her food, Nontshisekelo was walking in her direction, with her newfound friend's hand in hers while his family stood at a comfortable distance, watching and smiling. "Bye," was all the boy said as he unclasped his hand and turned to go back to his family. Nontshisekelo tucked into the food that Qhamukile had laid out for her in orderly piles on the lid of the picnic bag, now serving as a tray.

The clouds were gathering. The wind began to blow. Qhamukile looked at her watch. "Ok baby, five more minutes and we are out of here."

"Can't I play again when I finish eating Mama, please, please, please?"

"Nontshi no, you promised me, remember."

"Just once, one push on the swing."

"I said no, and you know you shouldn't even be asking. What's his name?"

"Who?"

"The boy you were playing with."

"I don't know."

Qhamukile smiled, tidied up and pulled her pouting daughter up by her hand. They walked back to the car and soon they were heading south again, the small town of Ladysmith beckoning.

"Please tell me a story, Ma."

"Kwasukasukele," she began.

"Cos' cosi," Nontshisekelo responded typically.

"Kwakukhona," she continued as she rifled through her brain files for a story. This traditional structured way of starting a story was very helpful, she thought for the first time. It's much longer than "Once upon a time there was a..." She had difficulty thinking of a story to tell. It's odd telling a story to someone whose face you cannot see. She had never done this before.

"Simhlabe ngogozwana."

"Ma, I'm waiting, you are supposed to start now."

"Which story do you want to hear?"

"The one about a frog, you haven't told that one in a long, long time."

"UNanana boselesele?"

"Yes, yes, that one."

Qhamukile began to tell the story, slowly, with all the animation she knew her daughter loved. Slowly she settled into the rhythm of watching the road, driving and telling the story. She had to repeat it each time it came to the end. After she had told it for the fourth time, and her daughter did not ask for a repeat, Qhamukile knew she was asleep. The Tugela tollgate appeared ahead, cars slowed down. From now on there was only one more tollgate, and they would be home.

Rita came back to her mind. She started to feel like an irresponsible friend. It's not enough to be the safe-keeper of her dagga. Maybe she should speak to their other friends so they could hatch a plan. She would never be able to forgive herself if Rita became a confirmed addict right in front of her eyes. She should stop being so lackadaisical about it. Isn't this what friends were for? What if the police heard about her safekeeping role? In fact, it was a very dangerous thing to be doing. An idea came to her. She should start by telling Rita she could no longer keep her dagga in her house. That would help open up the discussion. Yes, that should do it. Then she could plan with their three close friends. What had possessed her to agree to hide the stuff for Rita in the first place?

The clouds had darkened the sky by now, and it began to drizzle. By the time they reached the Mooi River tollgate, it was pouring and misty. Qhamukile remembered that even in the taxi times, this Mooi River area was notorious for thick mist and accidents. She drove with the lights on, more cautiously than before. As she paid at the Mooi River tollgate, she smiled and joked with the cashier, feeling good about a journey that was about to end. The thick tall forests that flanked the road on the northern parts of Pietermaritzburg complemented her mood. Mist steamed through the trees to greet the clouds as if awaiting an artist.

She pulled up outside her mama's gate forty-five minutes later than she had estimated. Although it had stopped raining, the wet roads had slowed her down a great deal as she approached the city, through the winding roads. Her mama walked to the gate as soon as she heard the car stop. She had a smile as bright as Qhamukile remembered. But so did the neighbour, MaMkhize, who talked more than Qhamukile's mama. She exited her gate, and entered her neighbour's gate without an invitation, right behind Qhamukile and Nontshisekelo. She even grabbed Nontshisekelo's bag out of Qhamukile's hand. But as always, there was sunshine of a smile on her face.

Once they were sitting in the living room, Qhamukile handed MaMkhize the Tupperware container full of banana muffins. She opened it immediately and smiled.

"How did you know I like these?"

"Oh Auntie, have you forgotten what you said the last time I was here?"

"What did I say, remind me?"

"You said I should never visit again without bringing you something."

They all laughed. Mother and daughter exchanged knowing glances.

"Qhamukile, you are now on the road."

"What do you mean Auntie, on the road, road to what?"

"Success my girl, success. This is how it starts, with beautiful cars. On our street, the whole street, who else has a car, who, tell me?"

Qhamukile eyed her mother, who responded with an embarrassed half-smile. She was tired and needed to rest. Her eyes wanted to close.

MaMkhize spoke first: "Nontshi, where is Nontshi? She must go and play with my grandchildren. They have been waiting to see just how she has grown. They haven't stopped talking about her since we heard you were coming."

Her mama's voice managed to claim some airtime.

"Qhamukile, go and rest in the bedroom, my child. After driving for so long, you must lie down for a while. Nontshi will go and play next door while I talk to MaMkhize. O, Qham'qham, Nontshi has really shot up like grass, hasn't she?"

Qhamukile gathered her handbag, took a book out of her bigger bag and walked to the bedroom. She closed the curtains, slipped out of her clothes and relaxed between fresh-smelling sheets. Her eyes closed and she smiled at the realisation that she had achieved another first. She took a mental walk through her list: Nontshisekelo – a personal and private first; voting two years ago – a first she shared with millions; the management position a year ago; then the car, a month ago.

Softly it started to rain again. The rain would help her fall asleep, but she did not know if it would last long enough. She needed to help it. She debated between reading her novel and responding to the surprising warmth, the creamy wetness she felt between her thighs.

Running

I'm a runner. That's the role I've given myself. A sub-role, if you like. I run from the plenary room to the rooms for small groups, to prepare them. I run from these rooms to the office to fetch and deliver messages and requests. I take children from the playroom to their mothers and vice versa (there are three toddlers and one on the breast). I run to call for technical help, something we seem to need often. Even the electricity in this hotel has a mind of its own. I run from the conference venue to our makeshift office, my hotel room, when we need to replenish stock. Yesterday I ran all the way to a taxi, and we drove to the nearest chemist to get anti-allergy medication after a comrade reacted to no one knows what. The doctor said my running made a big difference.

As a team we call ourselves the AST – the "administrative support team". I was asked to join when a comrade fell sick. There are five of us. I feel privileged to be working with such women. Accomplished in their professions, steeped in the organisation's politics, respected, women of integrity. All of them much older than I am, in their forties and fifties. That's why I chose to do the running bit; they are not as quick on their feet as they are with their brains. I have learned so much in just a week of preparations.

This conference. Well, this conference is history in the making. As an AST, we are the mechanics. We are the oil, or the nuts and bolts of the train to liberation. We've been talking in the team about the potential historical significance of this conference. Who knows, maybe ten years from today South Africa will be free. MK, the people's army, will have struck a heavy blow to the apartheid regime, freeing the country. Freeing us all.

I suspect the leadership is hiding certain facts. Why have they started preparing a constitution? They know something we soldiers don't. Maybe freedom is closer than we can even imagine. What with all these delegations from South Africa arriving in Lusaka, holding secret meetings with our leadership and then returning home. We are on the brink of something, something significant. I can feel it.

That's the other reason I am so proud to be part of this conference. As a soldier you don't get to hear much. The camps are claustrophobic. Here in the Zambian capital, news flows. I doubt the leadership likes that.

I've become a civilian. I'm a bit conflicted by that, actually, because as a trained soldier of the people's army, I should be with the other soldiers, preparing for a military takeover. Besides, there are so few women soldiers. I love the action, the discipline, the precision, the myriad skills, the versatility. Philosophically speaking, everyone in this movement matters, everyone has a key role to play. But hey, for me, the underground army is it.

My running role at this conference is similar to my role as a soldier. But being a soldier at a women's conference is unique. I'm moving between the two pillars of our struggle, mass political mobilisation and the armed struggle. This conference brings in another dimension, the international mobilisation, and I am a part of it. When I think of it this way, my conflict fades away.

The women of the ANC have decided to revise the draft constitution in order to make it non-sexist. That's why we are all here, one hundred and twenty of us, and only fifteen men. Seeing all these women in the flesh, in one place, made my pores sing a love song for my country. The names on the registration forms are now bodies I can touch. When I heard everyone introduce themselves yesterday during the opening session, I was humbled. It was a pleasant surprise to hear where they all come from, the work they do for the ANC in all those countries. With such an ocean of experience we have a right to call ourselves the "government in waiting".

Yesterday went much better than I expected. I ran from morning till late in the evening, but I was very disappointed by the service we got from this hotel. They are riding on the wave of long-lost fame, but I can't deal with such inefficiency. The conference venue is far from the hotel's administrative office, so I found myself running up and down to get the support we need from them.

At the end of the day, the AST came together for evaluation and prepared a summary of the day's proceedings. We smoothed out some administrative glitches by meeting with hotel management. Nomazwi, our team leader, was so direct with them, I know today will be better.

At 7am sharp, we arrive. The biggest room, named after President Kenneth Kaunda, is the main meeting-room for the four days of this conference. For group work we have five smaller rooms named after Zambia's colonial masters, whose claims to "discovery" I know not.

Nomazwi is clear: "We have to ensure that the curtains are on their hooks before we draw them open for day two. That's what working behind the scenes is about." We do our work with Nomazwi's guidance. Even with the improved service, I still run a few errands before we start. When the delegates walk through the door, we are ready at our table at the back of the plenary room. The conference starts promptly at 9am.

Today's agenda is more stimulating than yesterday's. We are getting into the content details of non-sexism. The more interesting, practical things. Yesterday we focused on contextual issues, concepts I know well. I hope I'll be able to listen to some of today's sessions. I want to listen to Comrade Lungile from Washington. Her paper, "Making Town Planning Non-sexist: A Model for the New South Africa", promises to be educational. It's the most unusual thing to choose to talk about. I'm curious. She is the first woman town planner I know.

I'm excited as we walk out for tea. Comrade Lungi is the first speaker after the tea break. When we are all back in the plenary session and Comrade Mapule, the chairperson, introduces Comrade Lungi, my anticipation heightens.

Someone taps me on the shoulder, indicating with his head I need to step outside. It's a man I know well by now, one of the hotel staff. I step out, closing the door as gently as he had opened it. Just outside the door is Comrade S'bu. He works in the Department of Information and Publicity.

"Comrade, I need to deliver an urgent message to all the conference delegates. Please tell the chairperson I need to interrupt." I notice the piece of paper in his hands. It's shaking. I look into his eyes and know that whatever it is, it's dead serious.

"Come, comrade." I usher him into the plenary room. I bend to tell Nomazwi what's happening and beckon S'bu to come with me. We walk next to each other down the middle of this plenary room to the stage where the two speakers and Comrade Mapule are sitting.

"The fourth section is on spatial concepts and processes. Here I assert that women's freedom is intricately interlinked with the physical spaces constructed around us."

Comrade Lungi flips the white cue card under the small pile in her left hand. I stare at her as I get closer to the stage. She has a black-and-white tailored suit made from kente fabric. An A-line skirt and a jacket. The white collar of her blouse reveals a slender neck, the colour of slightly toasted brown bread. As I get closer to the table, I conclude that she is beautiful. I suspect she is younger than me.

"In the fifth section, I propose options for creating safe spaces for women and for dealing with homelessness. To do this, I use examples mostly from the Scandinavian countries, where this has been achieved with varying degrees of success."

My heart beats faster, with a sense of agitation I don't understand. Walking next to Comrade S'bu is making me anxious. I wonder if Lungi has children.

"The sixth section looks at my proposal for the movement. As you can imagine, comrades, I have very strong feelings about this." She smiles as she says this. If she is disturbed by our approach, she is not showing it.

We step up the three stairs onto the stage. I whisper into Comrade Mapule's ear while Comrade S'bu stands right next to me. His left hand is now in his trouser pocket. His right hand still holds the piece of paper.

"In the last section I conclude with some crucial remarks, pointers really. Pointers I would encourage you all to take into consideration as this historic conference proceeds." Lungi looks at us, waits.

Comrade Mapule stands and addresses the delegates.

"Comrades, for those of you who have not met Comrade S'bu, he is from our Information and Publicity Department based here in Lusaka. Please pardon the interruption, he is bringing urgent news."

Comrade Mapule sits and Lungi follows suit. I squat at the end of the table. I've been squatting a lot during this conference, when it's my turn to carry the roving mike for the open discussion sessions.

Comrade S'bu approaches the podium, his right hand fisted in the air. "Amaaa-ndla!"

"Awethu," resounds in the large plenary room.

"Comrades, I will not waste your time. I know you are discussing important issues of our movement. We decided it would be folly to delay the delivery of this news. The enemy has struck. Once again, the enemy struck."

He pauses. An uncomfortable, long pause. He looks at the piece of paper in his hand and reads from it.

"This morning we received news from home. Comrade Reverend Vukile Dladla of the Methodist Church in Edendale, near Pietermaritzburg, in Natal, was gunned down this morning at about 7am. He was in his car. He had just finished an early morning meeting with comrades in the church. He died in the seat of his car. Five bullets were found in his body. Three were lodged in his head."

Silence. Then voices begin to murmur. How did they get the news so fast? Damn, these comrades are impressive! My head begins to spin.

"Comrades, once again we are reminded that the struggle continues. Comrade Reverend Vukile Dladla's death should be an inspiration to us all. His death is not in vain. His death *cannot* be in vain. The blood that was spilled this morning should remind us that the enemy is not sleeping. Amaaa-ndla!" Comrade S'bu steps aside.

The revolutions in my head gain speed. He is my relative.

He is our relative, family.

Mama's voice echoes in the distance.

He is the husband of my mother's younger sister's sister-in-law. I ask Mama what I should call him. Malume, she says.

They made a mistake with his surname. It's Mdladlane. It's a mistake people make frequently because Dladla is a more common surname.

After a confused pause, Comrade Mapule speaks, silencing the murmuring delegates.

"Comrades, can we all stand for a moment of silence to honour the fallen comrade." We all rise. A yawning silence engulfs the room.

They got the surname wrong. They got the surname wrong. I become conscious again only when I hear "Amandla!" and the response, "Awethu."

The delegates sit.

"Comrades, is there anyone in this room who knows the fallen comrade? Would they please say a word or two about him."

I feel a lump in my throat. It gets larger as my mind tries to guide me. "Talk, don't talk." "Talk." "Don't talk." Another Kaunda silence. The veins in my head are beginning to throb.

Mapule continues, now facing Comrade S'bu: "On behalf of the conference delegates, we'd like to thank you, Comrade S'bu, for bringing us the news, sad though it is. I trust that I speak on behalf of everyone in this room today. We shall never surrender. We are all in here today taking up the spear that Comrade Reverend has left. This conference is a testimony to that fact. Amaaa-ndla!" Comrade S'bu lifts his right fist, firm. Then he slowly moves off the stage. He walks out of the room, using a side door close to the stage.

Events unfold like a video in my head. I'm back in 1977, twelve years ago. Mama is doing her motherly duty. She gives me the number and address. She informs me it will be a good church to go to. That I should be well-behaved, visit the family, treat them as I would my own family. I must be helpful because they may need me. She reminds me they have younger children and that I should be a sister to them, just as I am with my siblings. I am nineteen years old, leaving home for the big city, Pietermaritzburg, to train as a teacher.

"Comrade Mapule!" A voice, accompanied by a hand in the air, almost shouts from the back. The speaker does not wait for a response. She walks through the chairs in no time, delegates watching. I recognise her immediately. We spoke at length when she came to the registration desk. Her complexion matches black olives. She is based in Moscow, a medical doctor. I don't remember her name. The chairperson waits, clearly giving her permission to speak. She stands in front, without getting onto the stage, speaks loudly without the microphone.

"Comrades, I am thoroughly disturbed by this news. I don't know Reverend Dladla, but as someone coming from Natal, the absence of anyone in this room who knows him is a clear demonstration of our movement's weaknesses."

By now the silence pounds, I'm aware of its rhythm.

Images continue to unfold.

I called him Malume, just as Mama suggested. He started by making time when we could be alone. He would drive me to the hostel after I'd had supper at their home. He would insist I didn't take the taxi. Auntie would agree. On some days I cooked supper, as Auntie did not enjoy spending prolonged periods in the kitchen. I was doing as Mama had instructed. I liked the children. I helped them with their homework. They liked me. They called me Sisi.

"The movement is failing the Zulus among us, comrades. People are dying in Natal. Our people. What has the movement done, so far, hhe? Can anyone here and now say what the movement has done about the special case in Natal?"

Malume always had a chocolate bar. He would let me step out of his car, then take a bar from his cubby-hole and say something like, "Thank you. Your aunt's health is going down and down. She really appreciates your coming over to cook for us." I would take the bar, thank him and disappear into the hostel. I didn't understand Auntie's health problem. She seemed fine to me. Secretly I thought she was just lazy, the complaining type, a hypochondriac, really.

I still wish to correct the small detail. His name is Reverend Mdladlane. Such a detail is important. I cannot find my voice. It's too late, anyway. The mood in the plenary room has changed. I should have spoken at that moment when I was invited to speak. I decide to let it go.

"This is a special case that deserves the movement's attention. I cannot sit here and watch us observe a moment of silence, and then continue as if nothing happened." Comrade Moscow finishes talking and walks slowly back to her seat.

The room begins to vibrate now, voices coming from all corners.

"I support the comrade that just spoke."

Heads turn to where the half-shouting voice comes from. Someone from the centre of the room is speaking right where she is seated. Then everyone begins to talk at the same time.

Someone from the back, close to my team's table, starts shouting. Her voice carries over every other voice. I don't recognise her face at all.

"Comrades, I'm based in Angola. As comrades from Natal we've been raising this issue with our commanders and commissars in the camps. We are soldiers, comrades. We want to be deployed back home to face the enemy. Our own people have now become our enemy. The state has turned them against us. We are soldiers. We *can* face Inkatha. What do our commanders and commissars say? 'Not yet, comrades. Comrades, that's not a good tactic. Comrades, our tactics need to match our strategy. Comrades, this is a very delicate matter. Comrades, we have to wait for…'"

"Order! Order, comrades!" Mapule speaks through the mike with a vehemence I never suspected she possessed. It dawns on me that this is why she has the job of chair.

The speed with which the actions unfold make my head feel bigger.

One day, about six months down the line, as he drops me off, he thanks me for having been helpful while Auntie has been so sick. He says he wants to thank me properly by doing something special.

Auntie has been in hospital for a week. For the first time I believe she is really ill. I have done the best I can to make her and the children comfortable. My schoolwork has suffered, though. I have been spending far too much time away from the hostel.

I tell him it was nothing. Auntie is like Mama to me. I did exactly what I would have done with Ma.

It takes time before the Kaunda room responds to the plea for order.

Mapule waits for silence to settle before she speaks.

"I know this is hard for us all, comrades. I may not be from Natal but I know the pain the comrades must be feeling…"

"It's time for action. Now!" a voice bellows from the left side of the room. It's a male comrade.

Mapule interjects, "Comrade, order! You have observer status during this conference."

"As I was saying, comrades," Mapule starts again, "The issue of escalating violence in Natal is undeniably critical. However, this conference is focused on something else. Something I know is close to all our hearts, a non-sexist constitution, a route to women's liberation."

I'm already out of the car when he tells me about his idea. He asks if I've ever been to the Lion Park. I shake my head. He wants to take me there, on a Saturday when I don't have to worry about school. How generous, I think. Two of my friends have just been there, thanks to their boyfriends. They went there as a group, a foursome, for a picnic. They could not stop talking about the fun they had.

The doctor from Moscow stands to speak without permission from Mapule. "Therein lies the problem, comrades. Are women not dying in the state-sponsored, Inkatha-executed slaughter in Natal as we speak? Are women not victims of the state's violent machinery? Are women not dying, comrades? If we are here to discuss women's liberation, I say the current crisis in Natal deserves urgent attention from us. Us, women at this very conference."

I like the way she speaks. I agree with her. It seems that most of the delegates feel as I do. Many are nodding and making agreeing sounds.

"Amandla!" a voice shouts from the front row.

"Awethu!" the Kaunda room reverberates.

Comrade Mapule takes the mike in her hand and speaks again.

"Comrades, this is a plea. Such events are meant to destabilise us. The enemy knows that such news will distract our focus. It's an old trick. Do something to derail the energies of the forces that are against you, and you win. We cannot allow that to happen."

Silence descends again.

On the Saturday we agreed on, Malume arrives alone at the hostel to pick me up. I ask about the kids. He says it will just be the two of us. My treat. It's his expression of gratitude.

There's something in the way he says that that makes me feel ill at ease.

My friends are waving me goodbye from the stairs in front of the parking lot. They wish me a groovy time, and I relax.

Lion Park, here I come.

We take off.

Mapule continues, "I have two suggestions. First and very important, let's remind ourselves that in this movement, we are one. There are no Zulus, Xhosas, Sothos, nothing. Dividing us along tribal lines was also a strategy for the Boers. Let's remember that as we move forward, comrades. This is not a theoretical suggestion. Thinking differently is an active process. My second suggestion is predicated on this mind shift. Secondly, I'd propose that we put the Natal issue…"

"It's a crisis, comrades. A crisis."

I know her. She works in the Youth League offices. Very tall for a woman, with long braids that give her face a look of someone older. Names are hard to remember today, with so many faces to work with. Her loud voice quivers.

"Unless we start thinking about it that way, we will not give it the attention it deserves. We need a strategy that responds adequately to this crisis. Comrade Reverend's death is meant to remind us of that. It is not a coincidence."

"Order, comrade."

Mapule starts again.

"I suggest we add the Natal crisis to our agenda. This will mean extending the time. We already have a full agenda. We cannot cut it. So, comrades, we'll need to sacrifice. Stay on till late tonight. Let's plan to break for supper as stated on the agenda, take just one hour, and get back at 8pm sharp to focus on the Natal crisis."

"Elethu! I second Comrade Chair. Amaaa-ndla!" Doctor Moscow shouts.

The way she carries herself in her black conference T-shirt and black pants makes her pronouncements more believable. Maybe it's her sturdy body. Maybe it's the doctor in her. She has a presence, one that says "take me seriously".

"Awethu!"

I start to feel pins and needles in my legs. I rise from the squatting position I've been in, walk down the stage back to our admin table. Now I feel alone as I walk down the middle of the room, surrounded by all the delegates. By the time I reach the table and sit, the room is silent again.

The scenery stretches ahead as we drive. The road between Pietermaritzburg and Durban has hillocks that rise and fall for kilometers and kilometers on end. I am half-excited. Malume speaks a lot. He does not give me time to say much. He is talking about the family, then skips to his church work, then back to the family and the community he works with. Now and again he turns to look at me as if to see if I understand him. My eyes are fixed on the hillocks.

"I also second Comrade Mapule."

It's Nomazwi, our team leader. She stood up without me noticing. She is now standing right at the centre, in the aisle next to our table. Heads turn to face her. She would pass as a hospital matron, a kind and sensible one. Yesterday she told me she is a social scientist, teaches at a university in Namibia. Her Afrikaans sounds like that of the Boers back home. During our AST meetings, she slips in and out of it.

"Mapule is making a good point, comrades. I suggest we do as she suggests. That way we stay focused."

She steps back to her seat.

Someone shouts, "Amaaa-ndla!"

"Awethu!"

"Thank you comrades, we will now proceed. Comrade Lungi, back to you."

I notice the sign to the Lion Park and begin to look forward to the picnic. He turns into the park, pays at the gate and begins the slow drive into the enclosed wilderness.

When Lungi speaks again, I look up and pay attention. I realise that her voice has a husky ring to it that makes you want to listen. Even from the back of the room she looks distinct, the black and white kente cloth adding a layer of elegance to her frame.

"Thank you, Comrade Mapule. In the interest of time, comrades, I propose that I skip the first … hmm … let me see. In the first section I was going to give you a broad, very broad brushstrokes really, on the history of town planning worldwide, but zooming in on philosophies and theories of planning. Ok, I'll skip that section. My paper is in your files…"

The Kaunda room begins to move. Delegates feel around for their files.

I am surprised the transformation is so rapid this close to the highway. The gravel road forces the car to slow down, even slower than the recommended speed. It's very dry. Trees look unhealthy, starved and sparse. There isn't much grass. I ask about the lions.

He turns, puts his left hand on my thigh, stares into my face, slowing the car down further. His left hand moves to the inner side of my thigh.

I freeze.

"Read that when you have time. I'll also skip the second section, but suggest that you read that thoroughly because I delve into crucial issues: heritage, values, African values and design as they relate to town planning. That section gives you the context that will be useful when we look at liberation of blacks and women."

He tells me that the lions are in their own enclosure, at the other end. That's where we will enjoy our picnic. The picnic spot is right in front of the lions.

The car stops. I look around, suspecting there's some wildlife to admire.

Then everything happens so confusingly, so unexpectedly swiftly, so violently.

Reverend Malume is all over me, his hands, his face. He is kissing me, breathing heavily, his hand is between my thighs, groping.

"The third section is on governance. I'll also skip that. It's an easy read. Hmm ... I'll start my detailed presentation with the fourth section, on spatial concepts. As I mentioned earlier when I outlined my presentation, I believe strongly that women's freedom cannot be separated from apparently benign issues like physical space."

It feels as if the whole car is rocking as he manages to hurl me onto the back seat of the car. I don't know how and when he lowered the back of the seat. I see him, his changed face, as he keeps looking fiercer and fiercer.

His body is heavy on mine. He keeps lifting it off as he instructs me to undress while he unzips his trousers.

I cannot hear everything he says between his groans. All I can focus on is how to get from under his body and out of the car.

My left hand has found the door handle. I pray the car is not locked.

"So, comrades, I want to start this section by doing a short exercise. I hope the exercise will also get those of us whose eyes are closing to wake up."

Some delegates laugh. Lungi smiles.

"I need you to sit in groups of five. Let's move quickly into groups, then I will tell you what do to next."

I see his penis, black and rod-like, spearing through.

I panic.

He moves off me. I see he needs room to undress properly.

I use this moment to pull the handle down. The door flies open.

With all my might, I push him away, wriggle, roll and throw myself onto the gravel. I cannot believe I am out of the car.

I get up and run. I run into the wilderness.

I stay on the road. I pray for another car to appear.

When I turn back, there is a car. His.

"Are you in dreamland, Comrade Zodwa?" Nomazwi pokes my arm with her forefinger and a smile. "We don't have to move, there's five of us." My team is looking at me. The whole room is abuzz as delegates rearrange themselves into groups.

I can't do this. I just know I cannot do this.

"Comrades please, you have to excuse me. I have to, I have to run, I mean, I have to go to the toilet."

I don't wait to hear what they have to say. I stand up, push the door open and run out and away, to my room.

I run faster and faster as his car gets closer. The plan in my head is clear. I will run until there's another car in sight. The wild animals can do as they please. I want to see him and his Christian conscience watch me getting eaten up.

I run.

I run.

I run around buildings, not through their corridors. When I arrive at my block, I take the stairs instead of the lift. I take some of them two at a time. I hold firmly onto the rail with each step. I stop only to catch my breath. I reach the fifth floor and turn left. My room is the second room after the stairs. I am grateful I volunteered to have it double up as an office. It seemed logical, for a runner. I share it with boxes, files, books, T-shirts, stationery. Everything the AST needed stored for the conference.

I look back. I notice another car approaching. My plan will work. The road is too narrow for cars to overtake. When the other car is right behind him, I stop running. He pulls up next to me.

"Get in the car. Have you lost your mind, Thixo mntwanandini!"

Panting, I open the back door and get in. He drives on without another word. I look back.

The car behind us follows. There are three passengers.

He picks up speed, far more than the allowed maximum.

I sit on my bed.

I stare at the conference paraphernalia. Then, I begin to sob.

By the time we drive past the lions' enclosure, swirls of dust follow us. I can't see anything behind us. He drives through the main gate. We reach the highway. We face Pietermaritzburg again. I sigh.

I have an irrepressible urge to tidy up, rearrange things into piles and rows.

I begin with the T-shirts. I re-fold. I re-pack.

I cannot stop crying, but things have to be in order before I decide what to do next.

Room for my Shoes

PHOTOGRAPHERS ARE THE reason I am here early this morning. Their pictures of suns rising from so many and varying horizons have been my inspiration for years. I've decided to come and record my emotions as the sun rises from behind the dark blue seas.

The sea looks agitated. The waves appear to be rushing to the shore at an anxious speed, one I have not seen in the few days since our arrival on this island. But then we have only come to the beach in the afternoon. Maybe this is the pre-sunrise rhythm. Amazing how much light there is already without the sun being up yet. Its rays open up like a gigantic deep-red fan above the sea and find a home in the sky. No wonder photographers are so obsessed with sunrise. It's one of nature's free theatrical performances.

It was a relief to finally find a working title for my mission: "Feeling Sunrise". People say the sea holds mysteries and secrets and wonders and many other indescribable things that mortals will never understand. So I've decided I will handle sunrise and the sea in my own way, a way that I understand well – emotions. They speak to me better than most people I have known, particularly Baba, the most emotionally inarticulate person I know. In part, my mission is to show Baba that emotions are not to be analysed. They are not to be seen as a source of embarrassment either.

They are to be felt, acknowledged, publicly if needs be, but most of all, they are to be embraced.

After five years of learning to live with Baba in his country, I think am finally beginning to understand him, learning how to communicate with him. His indirect zigzagging way of speaking no longer frustrates me as much as it did when Mama and I first arrived in South Africa. I am learning to find a straight path in the midst of his misty conversations.

"Luntu, my daughter, your father is a man learning how to be a father for the first time in his life. And he is old." I can hear Mama's voice, her standard response to my complaints. And Baba: "Ntombizoluntu, my child, rivers never decide for themselves which way to flow. The turns and twists they take are decided elsewhere, an elsewhere that's completely unknown to them. And when they do connect somewhere, where they could not have predicted, they rejoice at this congregation and proceed with their journey."

But Baba, you and I are not rivers.

Why am I thinking about all this now when I should be watching the sun? I can even see the smile that always decorates Baba's lean long face. His glossy teeth create a blooming flower of a smile. To think that there were so many, many times when I was not even sure that Baba and I were talking about the same thing. Then Mama would say, in typical style: "Luntu my daughter, be grateful you are now like other children, you have a father. Just imagine how our lives, your life, would have turned out if we had continued to believe that he had died in the camps?"

Ntombizoluntu positions herself comfortably on the rock before tugging her bag from behind her back and putting it under her head to work as a pillow. A rock against which to lean and another one on which to sit comfortably; what a perfect find. She feels a sense of tranquility as she imagines what colours the sea will turn as the sun rises. Her parents are still sleeping back in the holiday bungalow. She slipped a note under their door informing them she was going out to watch the sunrise. She is tempted to take off her Adidas running shoes, but the water might still be dreadfully cold.

A mad rush of water promptly washes over her shoes and wets her demin pants up to her calves before she can even jump to stand on top of the rock.

The sea is so close, it looks as if someone or something has pushed it from behind, from the horizon. She searches for the sand. It is gone. She looks up for signs of the emerging sun. Gone! Clouds of a whitish-greyish hue have covered the horizon. She turns, abandoning her notebook and flask behind, grabs her bag and jumps, amidst this confusion, onto rocks that march farther and farther away from the shore.

She turns to look again at the sand, and notices that the water has risen. She cannot even see the rock she was sitting on a few minutes ago. She begins to walk, looking for another rock to sit on. And she sees a rush of water from her right, approaching at a speed she had not imagined possible. She starts running, the water rushing behind. She runs faster and faster until she reaches a clump of shrubs. She recognises this; she had followed the path through these bushes on her way to the beach earlier. She tries to find the path again. It's hard work forging through these shrubs and sand. She is grateful she is wearing her tough demin pants. She decides to walk on, and fast. For the first time, she tunes in to the sound of the sea. Having been so focused on how it looked and the sun that was to emerge from behind it, she is surprised that her senses are capable of such adaptability. The sea roars. She thinks her hearing has lost its accuracy. She feels her heart missing a beat. She begins to run again. She wishes the path would appear in front of her.

Something is going on. Something is going wrong. She turns. It's much darker behind her now than it is in front. But something else has happened. Water is now seeping through the shrubs and flowing in her direction. She lets out a scream that shocks her. She silences herself with her right hand over her mouth. She does not know how to silence her heart: it is beating so loudly she thinks she may go deaf from it. Then something really goes wrong, the water floods her already wet shoes, and she falls, more from the shock than for any other reason.

She crawls for a few steps. Senseless as this feels, it comes naturally, as if to prepare her body for the run she knows she has to make if she is to be safe from the sea that has lost its mind. Then she rises, her hands dripping with grains of sand. She has scratches, two of which are bleeding like paper cuts. The water begins to sound like a hundred snakes hissing. She dares not look back. And she runs, awkwardly. In a surprisingly short while, she is on dry land.

With relief, she turns, slowly. It is now darker than when she last looked. This is a sea storm flowing over the land, she thinks. She wonders what happened to the fishermen she thought she saw from a distance when she first arrived. And what about the people out at sea? She notices the wind. It feels so heavy, it is blowing her inland. She turns around to walk with the aid of the wind, trying all the time to see the houses she knows need to start appearing. She walks faster, but no houses take shape. I must have come in the wrong direction, she thinks. Yes, I could not find the path. But keep walking and running, there's bound to be more land. It is getting darker and darker. She tucks her bag more firmly over her shoulder and begins to run. She trips over something and falls, again.

When her hands land on the ground or what ought to be the ground, she feels a body. She looks, with disbelief turning to panic, as she realises that she has tripped over the boot of a body. She picks herself up with lightning speed. What is a body doing lying here? It looks like a man's body. The clothes suggest he is a soldier. The ubiquitous military attire that young people and fashionistas have turned into hip gear. But this body is dressed in the real thing, the boots and the cap and ... and the gun. This is the AK47 she has seen on TV countless times. She is tempted to bend over and touch it but, her eyes lead her to another body and another and another.

Drops of rain pour over her body with a suddenness that makes her reach for her bag. This is no ordinary rain, she thinks. It's as if the sky has just opened up and let out a flood onto the earth. She fumbles through her bag for her cell phone. She panics. How does she keep safe standing between dead bodies at the start of a storm? Maybe they are not dead. What if they are not dead? She fumbles for her cell phone. She turns her bag inside out to allow the phone to fall out. *Even if it falls onto a dead body, I have to find my cell phone.* Nothing falls from her bag.

The rain is falling harder now, the kinds of drops that feel like an assault on the skin. She is grateful for the long-sleeved jacket she threw over her T-shirt at the last minute. Her head, recently shaven, takes the full force of the storm. But she can feel her body beginning to soak from the inside. She realises she has just been standing while looking for her cell phone. The best thing is to keep walking.

But how does one walk through dead bodies, or almost dead bodies? No, bodies on the ground. Men's bodies. How can she be sure they are all men's bodies? Does she wish to know? Dead bodies are dead bodies. None are moving, although she cannot be sure even of this, because she dares not check each one. Now she carefully looks for spaces between the bodies where she can place each foot. The right one. Then the left one. This forces her to walk in a zigzag fashion that even her father's speech pattern could not match. Keep walking, she thinks. The bodies seem to be packed closer and closer as she looks for room for her shoes.

The best thing to do is to think about something else, she tells herself. She just needs to do this mechanically, find space for a shoe, and move on. It's not so bad. None of the bodies have moved. As long as she chooses spaces carefully, she can just focus on that while her mind stays blank. That way it will be easier, and it will soon be over.

"What do you think, Luntu? Your father says we can longer plan surprises for you; you are truly a young woman now, and so you should choose where we go this holiday."

"Ma, Baba will not come, just like last year and the previous year, something will come up at work and he will cancel."

"Well, ask him yourself. He promised me that this holiday would be a special one. We are celebrating your 'BA with distinction!'" She said this last bit imitating me.

"What's the budget? How far can we go? For how long?"

"He has promised me a maximum of ten days. And the other condition is that we go to a holiday place in South Africa, because he wants to see and learn more about his own country." Baba never stops reminding us that he is never leaving South Africa ever again.

"Ma, you know exactly where I would like to go this time if Baba is coming."

"I'm a really committed mother, child, a good mother should always make it her duty to understand her child, particularly as there's only one."

"There you go again."

We laughed. I was excited. I suspected that Baba's brush with death three months earlier was the real reason he did not intend to miss this holiday. Doctor's orders. Why do politicians need doctors to instruct them on such simple things?

Her head turns with a jolt, she heard something, someone; a human voice on her right. But the thunder swallows all other sound. She calls out: HELP! HELP!

He is far away. The mist is not helping, but Ntombizoluntu is almost sure she can see a man, a tall man. He is walking as slowly as she is, as if he too is having to find room for his shoes amidst the corpses. His face is also bent downwards, his arms flailing at his sides, clearly to help him balance. Ntombizoluntu cannot believe that these motionless bodies stretch that far.

HELP! HELP! HELP!

Her voice echoes weirdly. She feels like a ventriloquist, another voice echoing in her throat. This man is not going to hear her, she thinks. One shoe between a man's legs and the other in a space between this man and the curve of his neighbour's stomach. For the second stupid moment she thinks: my lost cell phone.

Then a thought crosses her mind. She quickly takes off her jacket and begins to wave her hand above her head in circular motions, fan-like. That should attract his attention. She is terrified of shouting again. She stands there, legs astride, waving her navy-blue corduroy jacket. This feels stranger than walking among corpses. The man doesn't look up. He just walks. He seems to have a better rhythm than Ntombizoluntu. As if his corpses are not so close to one other. But he has corpses there for sure, she thinks, or he wouldn't be facing down.

She abandons the idea and decides to keep walking. But this finding space for her shoes is not walking. Just as she is thinking that, she notices the next face facing upwards. It's a woman's face. No mistaking that. Her eyes and mouth are open. Blood trickles down her left cheek.

Ntombizoluntu realises the sun must have come up because even though the rain drops are no longer that big, its lighter everywhere. No! She panics. It was better when she could not see their faces, or any details, for that matter. She can see more clearly now. Almost every body has blood somewhere, on the combat clothes each one is wearing. How could they be fighting so close to the beach? She throws her sight further and further, and as far as she can see, there are mounds and mounds of bodies in as many contorted positions. And still no one moves. Guns and what looks like grenades are strewn amidst the bodies. And bags, in military green, like the clothes. She finds room for her shoes and walks on, beginning to cry. Her tears block her view. She does not bother wiping them away. She just allows herself to weep and walk. Weep and walk.

And then a better idea hits Ntombizoluntu. She puts her jacket around her neck, ties it loosely and begins to clap her hands as loudly as she can. HELP! Clap. HELP! Clap. HELP! Clap, clap. Her voice echoes and she notices that the rain has stopped. She is now sobbing aloud in between the claps and the shouts. The horizon lightens up now and again as if the storm is moving far ahead, but when she looks down, there are just bodies.

Then she hears an unmistakable sound: a baby crying, as if in response to her clapping. It seems close by, maybe ten more steps in the direction right ahead. Her heart misses a beat. A live baby among so many motionless bodies! Maybe when she holds it in her arms she will stop crying and stop being so afraid. Her chest is pounding harder than she has ever felt. Nothing in her whole life has prepared her for this. She decides to speed up to where the sound is coming from. She lifts her left foot, hooks through an arm and falls face first on top of three bodies. "Why on earth would you give up your comfortable holiday bed for these rocks?"

The sun is out and a woman, possibly her age, is standing in front of Ntombizoluntu, holding a large transparent bag full of sea shells.

She clutches her bag, smiles, and scrambles to her feet.

"Oh sorry, I did not see you come."

"How could you, with your eyes closed?"

Ntombizoluntu smiles shyly, excuses herself and starts walking briskly back to their holiday bungalow. *I have to tell my parents about this dream.*

When she finishes talking, she takes a deep breath. Her parents are staring at her. Her mother reaches out, put her hand on her daughter's right thigh. "Relax Luntu, it was just a dream."

"How many times have I told you to stop reading that TRC report? It's not good for your soul." As Baba spoke, he rose from his garden chair, and gave his wife and daughter his back as he strolled into the lounge. "It's news time."

Baba has never spoken to me like that, ever. Not only was he direct, he had a reprimanding tone in his voice. Ntombizoluntu thought about this many times that day.

People of the Valley

THIS IS *TALK to Thuli at Twelve*. Sanibonani Sanibonani, you people of the valley. Welcome to your day's favourite programme, *Talk to Thuli at Twelve*. This is your loyal Vukavuka Community Radio station, 101 FM. Kusinwa kudedelwana bakithi. Out goes Bheki Mavuso, in comes Thulisile Thabethe. Out goes one-way traffic, in comes two-way traffic. Out goes information, in comes conversation. I'm your host at twelve, and for the next hour you and I mlaleli will ta-a-a-alk. If you're tuning in for the first time, welcome dear listener. During the next hour all we do is ta-a-a-alk. We talk about any topic at all as long as it affects residents of the valley, us. Unfortunately today, I say unfortunately, the topic for today was chosen by the universe and not by you people of the valley. I'm sure you all agree with me that today we have no choice but to talk about the news that broke this morning at about 6am. Sad news though it is, it's our news, our community, our issue, therefore for us to understand and solve or simply talk about.

Now if you have not yet heard the news, let me break it to you gently. Those of you who are regular listeners know that I try to walk every morning. This morning as I was getting ready to say goodbye to my mother and walk out of the house, the news broke. My mother leaves the house promptly at 6.30am so we always say our goodbyes when

I leave for my walk at six. When I get back to the house, it's just her chickens, my goats and myself. I was tying my laces when I heard it.

Last night apparently the police arrested Matron Langa. I don't think there's anyone in the valley who doesn't know Matron Langa. She came to the valley fifteen years ago and has done amazing work at Philani Community Health Centre, a 24-hour clinic, first of its kind in the whole region. Children who were born when she first came are now going to high school. She delivered many of them, many of us, I should say. I myself was only ten years old when she first came to the valley. Today I speak to you as a radio talk show host. Matron Langa had the vision that led to the renovation, upgrading and extension of Philani Clinic. She knew how to talk *to* government people. She knew how to talk *for* her people. She was tireless in her efforts. She came from the other side of the mountain but once she was in the valley, she became one of us, beautiful people of the valley. Some people actually say that without her, we would still have a small clinic that only opens during the day. The staff has increased from four to twenty. There is a three-bed maternity ward and a casualty unit that opens all night. We even have an ambulance now that we share with people of the Njoko clan on the other side of the mountain.

The lines are buzzing already, but let me first finish the story. Allegedly someone tipped off the police and they went and raided Matron Langa's home. They found a freezer full of women's placentas. Yes, the police had the organs tested and it's been confirmed they are placentas, most of them full-term ones. For those young people who have no idea what a placenta is, let me explain it to you as it was explained to me. When a baby grows in its mother womb, it connects with its mother through the umbilical cord, *inkaba* in isiZulu. That is what midwives cut soon after the baby has come out. Now that cord is the extension of the placenta, a flat mass of tissue that looks a bit like the liver *isibindi*, but not smooth like the liver. It's that organ that helps to attach the baby to the inside of its mother's womb. With a normal birth, this placenta comes out of the woman soon after the baby has come out. Now I am told midwives have a system for throwing this thing away. Apparently they are required by law to throw this away, dispose of it. But apparently in this case Matron Langa took these placentas home and put them in her freezer. Staff at Philani are in shock. Some say it cannot be true. No one knows why. She is in police custody as we speak, and I have confirmed this information. I spoke to the station commander. Matron says she is not saying a thing until her lawyer arrives.

Now, people of the valley what do you have to say to this? Shocking news indeed. Call me on the number that you now know so well, TTTAT for *Talk to Thuli at Twelve*, let's hear your say. Yes, the lines have been buzzing, so I won't waste time. Yes, welcome Ma Duma.

Thuli Mtanami, nguwe lowo?

Yes, Ma Duma, yimi.

Listen here my child, I am your grandmother and you know I listen to you every day, I have been sitting here waiting for you to come on my radio. Was it last year when I called and said ubuthakathi busabaphethe abantu abamnyama? Remember? This is simple and straightforward. Matron Langa is a witch. Period. Why do you think she left her village? She never visits her people, do you know that?

No Ma Duma, but how do you know that she never goes home?

Thuli, my grandparents okhokho bokhokho ungizwa kahle, they were born here eVukavuka. When Vukavuka was a peaceful valley. We who have been here through our ancestors from the beginning of time know everything about everybody in this valley. Even this radio station of yours, we know all about it.

Thank you, Ma Duma. Let's hear what others have to say on this matter. Ma Duma has raised a few issues. If you've just tuned in, I am Thulisile Thabethe on your special talk show *Talk to Thuli at Twelve*, where we discuss issues affecting our community. And this is your favourite radio station, Vukavuka Community Radio. Next caller, yes BL, go ahead.

Thuli, I say this is a shame, this is a shame that has befallen our community and we need to do something about it. I'm not sure what, but this is a bad sign. When respectable people of the community start doing such horrible things it means one and one thing only, konakele, konakele, Thuli, bye that's all I wanted to say.

Hmm thank you, BL. People of the valley, do you agree with BL when he says, I think he was saying, that this incident is a sign that something bigger is wrong, this incident is – just as we say in the valley – the tip of the mountain?

Welcome to Vukavuka Community Radio, our next caller is Mxo, yes, Mxo. Talk to Thuli.

Hellow Thuli, thanks for taking my call. I am calling from the primary school eVulamehlo. I teach Grade Three and as I speak to you my children have left the school. At about ten a woman came to fetch all the children who were born at Philani. She says she wants the police to make Matron Langa identify their placentas.

What? Are you serious?

I am dead serious Thuli, half the pupils in my class have left and some of the other teachers have also lost pupils. Mrs Khanya our principal in fact asked me to call your show so you can appeal to the community to be calm about this situation. She is trying to manage the situation as best as she can. I tell you Thuli, it's chaos here. Some parents have started coming individually to take their children.

Identifying placentas to what end? What are they saying this will achieve?

Thuli, I also don't understand it very well, I've just been told that it's important. I think it's got to do with ancestors. Please Thuli, talk to the community. We need calm all round.

Now whoever thought that frozen placentas could create such panic! I can't believe this! Mxo, thanks for your call. We *are* talking and talking is one way of dealing with the problem. The lines have not stopped buzzing. Talk to me, our next caller is Masande. Yes, Masande.

Yebo Thuli. Ngingakhuluma ngolwakithi?

Khululeka Masande, khululeka here on Vukavuka Community Radio sikhuluma zonke izilimi. Lithini-ke elakho Masande?

Thuli, ngivumelana nalo othi konakele esigodini sakwethu.
Kwazi bani ukuthi wawuqala nini lomkhuba uMatron Langa?
Kwazi bani ukuthi zingaki izibeletho zabafazi bawo wonke
amathafa lawa eziphelele efrijini yakwakhe? Elami nje lithi akekho
umuntu ongenza into enje engaguli, UMatron Langa uyagula, ugula
ngekhanda? Sithi sinomhlengikazi nje kanti nguye qobo ogulayo.
Ngiyaphela lapho Thuli.

Wow, thanks Masande. Now that's an interesting
perspective. No one has said this so far. Masande says
only a mentally sick person can do what Matron Langa
allegedly did. But Masande also raises other questions. She
wants to know how many placentas are in that freezer.
She wants to know when Matron Langa started doing this.
Well, she makes me think: is the freezer full of placentas
only or are there other goodies in there? When I spoke
to the station commander, he said they suspected by the
way the freezer was packed that it was all placentas, but
he had no clue as to how many there were and refused to
even estimate. I believe they are waiting for the freezer to
defrost completely before a forensics expert can confirm
what all the goodies are. They are expecting one from the
city by three this afternoon.

I'm your talk show host Thulisile Thabethe, and we are
discussing the shocking news of Matron Langa's arrest.
Next caller, Njenje, is that Njenje?

Yebo Thuli. Uyabona Thuli, abathi uMatron uyahlanya nami
ngiyabavuna. The bigger question is how can we, all of us, have been
fooled by this person who came from the other side of the mountain,

made herself comfortable among us because we could not do things for ourselves, and now she has poisoned the whole valley?

Poisoned? What do you mean Bab'uNjenje?

Thuli ngithi isihlava sohlanya uMatron Langa, uyasazi isihlava? Before we know it the whole community will be rotten, just like her. A Matron who poses as a healer ends up poisoning the community what do you call that, hhe?

People of the valley, please, I know this is shocking for all of us, but let's try and come up with solutions not accusations! Let's ask questions if we must, but questions that will help lead us to answers. Calling Matron Langa names is not going to deal with our situation. Now, if someone – a nurse, or a doctor on duty, a midwife, anyone who really knows from Philani Community Health Centre is listening, please call Vukavuka Community Radio Station. I would like to know the step-by-step process that midwives and doctors are expected to follow when disposing of the placenta. Why do I want to know this? I think, well I hope, that an informed answer to this question will help us understand even in a small way why Matron did what she did. Maybe there is a simple answer. Maybe placentas can only be disposed of in bulk, for cost-effectiveness. We simply don't know at this stage. Next caller on the line, Libuyile. Talk to me Libuyile, you are calling from the secondary school Qhubekani.

Yes Sis'Thuli. As you know I'm like a regular caller on your cool show. I'm like responsible for our newsletter Vukavuka Valley Voice. *Needless to say Sis'Thuli, our school is also like in major like shock, but I'm like calling to tell you what my fellow students have decided to do. When you asked for solutions I thought I should like holla at ya, you know like tell you what we're doing.*

Go ahead Libuyile, that's so good to hear.

But before I go into that and I know you just said we need to stop with the accusing and find a solution but I like really need to put this out there. Sis'Thuli, don't you think it's like totally and utterly gross when you think about where she was keeping these things. I mean, I know like anywhere else and they would have gone rotten and smelled horrible but I mean this was her like freezer where she kept her food, her food Sis'Thuli. Can you imagine like every night going into your freezer and deciding to like take out your chicken breasts to defrost and having to like move aside thousands of women's bodily organs? Old bodily organs, I might add!

I hardly think it was anywhere near a thousand, Libuyile.

Ok, so maybe I'm exaggerating a little but still, iyuuuu!

Back to your solution, Libuyile. Let's hear it.

Ok, ok Sis'Thuli, the editorial team. We like held an emergency meeting, you know, to talk about this issue, neh. And our focus was what can we like contribute, so we like thought statistics would be cool. So like besides the regular reporting and releasing a special issue on this alone we're going to do a kinda survey, you know, research.

Hmm, I like the sound of that Libuyile, you go girl. Tell us more about your research, but please try and speed up or we will be running out of time.

Yes Sis'Thuli. Well the idea isn't fine-tuned yet but we were thinking we could do something like going to Philani and asking them like exactly how many kids were delivered by this matron and who they are, neh. When I think about it, any of my Grade Eight and Nine friends (I say Eight and Nine coz we're only a high school, remember) *could have been delivered by this woman and like had their placentas stuffed in a freezer. I mean, what's with that? Anyhoo, moving on. Then neh, we could go to those kids and interview them. Ask them questions like how they feel about their placenta being in like a freezer for so long. And whether they're not like totally grossed out. Now we're like expecting the majority of these guys and gals to be under fifteen, like you said. So when we see the completely miffed looks on their faces the next question will obviously be like whether they even know what a placenta is and whether they care.*

I like that, Libuyile. I like it very much. But please, please, call her Matron Langa. She is not "this woman", she continues to be Matron Langa whatever she had done. We prefer some respect on this radio station.

My bad Sis' Thuli, I'm just really peeved by this whole thing, so is the whole committee.

That's all right Libuyile, but my question to you is how's *that* gonna help the police investigation, the people of the valley, or even Matron for that matter?

Well Sis' Thuli, as said earlier the idea is not like exactly fine-tuned yet, neh, mara we're getting there. And we're determined to help in some way. People of the valley need to know that kids have brains and can make a major diff if you let us.

So tell me Libuyile, does your committee have money to do this research?

Hhayi six no nine, seven nes'bhamu Sis' Thuli, we'll find a way.

There you have it people of the valley, our young people also want to have their say. They want to make a difference. Libuyile, I wish you and your team all the best. Come back and talk to us at *Talk to Thuli at Twelve* once your research is on the go.

Ngiyabonga Sis' Thuli, bye. Thanks for listening, my chomies and editorial team will be so like excited.

Next caller, you're welcome Mrs Khuzwayo. This has to be such an interesting topic for people of the valley. The callers are so passionate today. Mrs Khuzwayo, you're on air.

Thank you, Thulisile. I want to ask the people of the valley two questions. One: how different is this Matron Langa story from the thousands of stories of rape of girls and women we hear about all over the country? Two: how different is Matron Langa's story from the deputy president's story of corruption and fraud? I say these cases are not different.

You will have to say more there, Mrs Khuzwayo.

Thuli, it's logic, Matron Langa is taking away women and children's dignity, in this case mere newborns. Isn't this what rapists do? Matron Langa is using her power to fool the people just like the deputy president.

Mrs Khuzwayo, the deputy president still has to go to court. He has not, I repeat, not been found guilty yet.

OK Thuli I get you, my apologies. Let me just say Matron Langa is just like all other people who are in power, in high positions all over the country, who fool the common people. They pretend to be someone they are not. Matron Langa has fooled us all. We thought we had an angel of a matron, now we know she is the devil herself.

But Mrs Khuzwayo, she has not been found guilty yet.

Point is Thuli, someone blew the whistle on her. Someone knew something we didn't know. I bet you it's one of her colleagues. Me,

I don't even want to know the disposal procedure, I just know that if there's someone who blew the whistle, then Matron Langa is not following the procedure. They knew something was freezing unprocedurally, illegally in Matron's freezer, and they told the police. Everyone working at Philani has to talk. It's time to tell the truth now.

Mrs Khuzwayo…

I bet you Thuli ngifung' aMaNgidi ephelele, a lot more people know something about this but one person was brave enough to tell.

Yes Mrs Khuzwayo, can you please…

And, Thuli, and, I'm about to finish, my theory is that she was selling these placentas to someone somewhere somehow. I mean, why else would she keep so many? She is getting rich on women's dignity and individual pride. How can anyone born in Vukavuka during the She-devil matron's time say where their umbilical cord is buried? That's us Thuli, that's just who we are as a people.

Mrs Khuzwayo –

No, honestly Thuli, everyone wants to be able to say with pride where their umbilical cord was buried. Don't you?

Mrs Khuzwayo, sorry, I am going to have to cut you off. The lines are buzzing, many people need to talk. We get your point about dignity but to call Mrs Langa a she-devil is uncalled for. Not on this radio station, please. Our next caller, yes, welcome to *Talk to Thuli at Twelve*. Jongiwe, you are next, talk to me.

Molweni, thanks Thuli, sana I am very, very surprised that so many callers are talking like this. The only person that has made sense to me so far is Mrs Khuzwayo. I think she is right about something, what if Matron Langa is in business, iphi ingxaki apho? Thuli sana, how many times have you yourself said on this radio station that women must stop complaining and start acting. Matron Langa saw an economic opportunity and acted. There's only one reason to keep so many of the placentas, to sell, you know sana, make money.

Jongiwe, so you are saying the matron should be left alone because we all have the constitutional right to make money anyway we like?

Thuli sana, let me ask you and your listeners a question, people throw away plastic bags right? Others collect these, cut them up and make items from them, and sell those items, you know floor mats, place mats, hats, right? Others collect them and create artistic pieces from plastic, right? They make money from what others consider waste. Now, who says it's illegal to use human waste in this case, placentas? Tell me Thuli, since when is that illegal?

I must say that's an interesting and fresh take on this issue. Thanks, Jongiwe. Listeners, if you have just tuned in, this is your favourite midday programme *Talk to Thuli at Twelve* on 101 FM. Jongiwe asked a pertinent question: what is wrong with Matron Langa using this economic opportunity, human waste? Our next caller is Sembathiseni, you are calling from the Gwinyamathe General Dealers, right?

Yes Thuli. As someone from the shop I also agree with the last caller what's her name.

Jongiwe. Her name is Jongiwe. Please go on.

Yes, Jongiwe. I actually take my hat off for Matron Langa. To me she is a hero of which I support. First she came to our Valley and changed things the way we had never imagined, aneh? Mos dan that's what the new South Africa is all about, neh, of which it's working for our khawntry. That's all I wanted to say.

Thank you Sembathiseni, brief and to the point, let's build the economy for the country. Next caller, yes Prettyboy. Did you say your name is Prettyboy?

Yes Thuli, it's just a nickname you know mos. Me, I want to argue a new point. If people are now agreeing that Matron was in business, who, tell me who, would want to buy placentas? To do what with them? Thuli, when people make statements I think they need to support them. Who would buy placentas, what are they useful for?

Prettyboy, pretty point. I take your point eh. Mrs Khuzwayo and Jongiwe, if you are still listening please call the station back again. I want to know what you think of Prettyboy's challenge. It's a simple point. If Matron Langa is trading in human organs, who might she be selling them to, in other words what's their value? If you've just tuned in, this is *Talk to Thuli at Twelve*, 101 FM. Next caller, you're on air Makwenzeke.

Thank you for taking my call, Thuli. I have been listening now for a long, long time. I think everyone is missing a very significant angle. I think it's sad that the people of the valley, my people, are so quick to jump to conclusions.

Makwenzeke, I have to interrupt you there, please won't you come to the point. What's your significant angle?

My angle, Thuli, is the most simple one, most sensible one, most matter-of-fact and practical one. Research. Thuli, a place as big as Philani Community Health Centre is an ideal place for researchers to do their work, right? And we live in a unique geographical area of

KZN province. I want to believe that there are peculiarities that are found only in our area that call for research. Agree?

I hear you. Proceed.

Matron Langa is the most senior person at this health centre, right?

Ja-ja.

So, who would be taking responsibility for research samples? Mrs Langa of course, right?

Now I think you have an interesting new angle there, Makwenzeke. Are you a health professional yourself?

No, I was just working for six months for a pharmaceutical company, and I know that they use clinics and hospitals a lot for information. They collect samples from large clinics and hospitals and use them to find answers to research questions.

Interesting indeed! Would you have any ideas of what answers could be sought from placentas?"

No Thuli, I don't know, but if I were to hazard a guess I would say it has to do with maybe genetic research, you know this DNA stuff everyone talks about. A placenta is located in a key position between the mother and her baby, so I think, I said I think, that's the kind of research they, someone, some pharmaceutical company may be doing.

Thank you Makwenzeke. A new angle indeed. The question remains though, supposing, just supposing that Makwenzeke is right, wouldn't the rest of the staff at Philani know about this ongoing research? Why would anyone tell on the Matron if she was doing what the last caller suggests? You are listening to *Talk to Thuli at Twelve*, 101 FM. Next caller, you're on air.

Thuli! Is that Thuli?

Yes caller, you are on air. Talk to me.

Can you hear me there?

Yes I said you are on air already. Talk nam.

Thuli! Is this the radio?

Bad, bad line I'm afraid I'm gonna have to cut you there. We have time for a few more calls. Mrs Mthethwa, you are next, please talk to me.

Thuli you know me, me I think there's a lot of truth in what the early, early callers were saying. You see I think people of the valley are losing their traditions. You know before these hospitals and clinics arrived, people had enormous respect for the placenta. They buried it ceremonially you know, there used to be a special ritual for burying the placenta.

Tell us what it was, please, Mrs Mthethwa.

Sorry Thuli even I don't know it, but my grandmother used to tell me that the reason so many people leave their homes and never return, some never even have the desire to return, is because they were never rooted properly in the soil.

People of the valley, if anyone knows the rituals of burying the placenta, please, please, please, give us a call before this show ends, and that's pretty soon. Now, can I ask every single caller waiting to speak to please keep it short. The lines have not stopped, everyone in the valley has something to say. So please be brief and come with a new angle. Next, Baba Mbonambi, you're on air.

Thuli, thank you for the time. You were still in napkins when Matron Langa arrived here. We used to listen to uKhozi radio. Your station is just three years old.

Baba Mbonambi we all know that, your point please.

My point is simple: people who are old enough still remember that this Matron Langa, when she came here, she came under a cloud.

Meaning?

Meaning two things, one: people said she is a Kwerekwere from Mozambique, that she changed her name and chose an easy one that she could pronounce. Two: people said, note I say people said, she had killed her husband in Mozambique. That's all I wanted to remind you young ones.

Wow, Baba Mbonambi. I don't know if I want to go there. Listeners, people of the valley, I feel I don't know what I feel. Any comments on what Baba Mbonambi has just said, eh? This is *Talk to Thuli at Twelve* on your one and only community radio station, the station for the people. Next caller on the line, Singabakho. Singabakho, I've always loved that name. Talk to me. Talk to us, Singabakho.

Firstly Thuli Mr Mbonambi is right about those rumours. They did circulate when she first arrived here. But hey, I also killed my husband after twenty years of violent abuse and numerous rapes that I reported to the police and the community over the years. That's why I won my case in court. I came to this valley to escape my community down there in the south coast. Some of them wanted me to go to jail. But that's not my point. My point is this: me, I think the other nurses at Philani Community Health Centre should come on radio and clarify things for us. There's far too many questions around this, we need clarity and facts before we can discuss. That's my request.

Great points there, Singabakho. Wow, thanks for sharing that personal story as well, Ma. Moving. Touching. In fact, I think we need to do a show, another show, on that topic, women who murder their husbands. Wheh! Very, very, moving! I agree and appeal to staff members at the Philani Health Centre to please call the station and give us their perspectives on this issue. I asked for this earlier, listeners want it as well. Principal MaNkosi on the line. Yes Madam Principal, you are on air.

Thuli, as you know I am the principal and owner of the creche, I am surprised that no one is talking about Matron Langa's human rights. I want to make one point, let's hear from a lawyer what rights Matron Langa has under such circumstances. First and foremost, what has she been charged with? What is the charge? Do you know if I am keeping dead rats in my freezer, do the police have the right to come and take me to the police station? For what, hhe? Thank you.

Good point principal, it reminds me that in fact my producer has been trying to get hold of Advocate Nomali Mnikathi, who is always ready to advise us on legal matters. She is in court and might call in soon. So, yes, we are going to go there. Next caller, Nomazizi. Nomazizi, talk to me.

Ja, thanks. I have this idea that sort of builds on that one by that caller who spoke about research. I would like to know what else is kept in freezers by all the nurses who work at Philani Health Centre. I have also heard many stories about people trading in human organs and researchers acquiring body parts without permission. If the police were to go and check all the freezers of the staff who live in that boarding house – how many are they, ten? – who knows what they would find? That's all I wanted to say, Thuli.

To the point, Nomazizi! I am going straight to the police station at the end of this show, by the way. Next caller, Phathizwe.

Me, I think we are being called upon to pray. We need to pray hard for this community. The primary school has been closed now. Children have all left, the gates are locked. And there is a long queue of people outside the PCHC gate and the security people are stopping people from jumping over the fence. I live right next to the school, and the PCHC is walking distance from there, I have just come from there. So, me, I just wanted to suggest Thuli that you close this show with a prayer. God bless you and the people of this valley. Amen.

Phathizwe, Amen there. We have time for the last two callers. To the point, please. Thathiwe, you're on.

I just wanted to say I agree with Phathizwe, but I think people should also pray for Matron Langa. But my point is simple, please warn the community Thuli, no one should be attacked during this whole confusion. No one! That's all, thank you.

Brief and the point! I couldn't agree with you more there, Thathiwe. Last and final caller, Njengelanga, you're our last caller on *Talk to Thuli at Twelve.* Let's hear your point. Njengelanga.

Thuli, that caller who told us she killed her husband, wow, what courage! I am curious as well about the rumours about Matron Langa. She has no children, no known relatives, we and when I say we, I mean us young people, mostly we just love her because we have known her all our lives. She just seems to have been here all the time, like the river and the mountain. So I wanted to suggest, Thuli, that when this whole fracas is over, invite her to the show. We love her, we will listen. Thanks, that's all I wanted to say.

People of the valley, this ends our show for today. This show will go down in history as the show during which phones rang non-stop from the first minute at twelve to this very last minute. My producer Musawenkosi is sweating. His fingers are numb from pressing the buttons. Thanks, Musa. To the rest of the technical team: Ndawoyethu, Dedanimabhunu, Velemazweni and Tholakele, as always: many thanks!

Wow, I have to breathe. I cannot even begin to summarise the main points of our show today. What a pity no one called from the clinic. It would have been great to get a perspective from someone working there. But we get it people of the valley, don't we? And we empathise. I imagine the clinic is pretty hectic as we speak. I'll make sure we speak to someone from the clinic tomorrow.

One more promise: I'll be back with you tomorrow at *Talk to Thuli at Twelve*. Nisale kahle. Nisale kahle, you people of the valley. This is your loyal Vukavuka Community Radio station, find us on 101 FM. I am Thulisile Thabethe at *Talk to Thuli at Twelve* signing off. Ngangezwe Ngubane coming up next. It's one o'clock.

The Weekend

The taxi stopped.

Phatheka, the older woman, unclasped her right arm, tapped the younger woman next to her on her left thigh, and said, "This is it."

They exchanged glances, gathered their handbags. The younger woman had a second bag, a plastic one from Kentucky Fried Chicken. They found their way to the sliding door of the taxi.

Once outside, Phatheka looked at the street pole, read the name and murmured, "Yes, this is it, Vilakazi Road." She looked at the time, reaching for a pendant watch on a silver necklace. She pulled it away from her chest, tilted her head backwards, squinted and read: *18:35 FRI.* The younger woman watched. Then they began walking to the left, up a steady gradient, hugging their handbags.

By the time they had crossed three streets, both were gasping. They stopped to rest. When their breathing had subsided, they walked on in silence. After the fifth street, a yellow house with a green roof and green palisade gate beckoned in a cul-de-sac. By now, it was the only house without lights on.

There were a few walkers, a handful of older children playing football, one on a bicycle. Darkness had ushered in the weekend. The gate was not locked. The younger woman, Zaba, let Phatheka walk in first. The green front door had a welcome sign and the name "Menzi's Boarding House" on it. Phatheka unzipped her bag, found the keys and unlocked the door.

"Someone is coming," Zaba whispered, touching Phatheka on the back, as if to stop her from opening the door. Phatheka was not deterred: "Whoever it is, they cannot be coming here. Menzi said business is bad these days. He has only two boarders this month, and they both go home on weekends." Zaba slid through the door hastily and shut it.

Phatheka flicked on the switch next to the door. The corridor lit up, displaying newly painted walls, plastic tiles on the floor. The walls breathed paint. The corridor had four doors on each side. The first door to the left was open, exposing the kitchen. The first door to the right was also open, showing the lounge. At the end of the corridor, directly opposite the front door, was another door.

They walked to the end of the corridor, stopped in front of the fourth door to the left. Phatheka, who still had the keys in her hand, unlocked the door. They went in. Phatheka put on the lights. Zaba shut the door.

As if on cue, they walked straight to the luggage that they had left in the house earlier that day. They freed their shoulders of their handbags, putting them down on their travel bags.

The bedroom had a queen-size bed against the wall to the right side of the door. A bedcover of large sunflowers spoke to the walls. Against the wall opposite the bed stood a wooden chest of drawers, the kind that makes you want to ask many questions. At the head of the bed was a black couch. At its side, a lean yellow wardrobe.

Phatheka removed her doek, folded it into a square and placed it on her handbag.

Zaba strode to open the only window, just above the chest of drawers. She spoke to herself: "I can't stand this paint." She pushed the window handles as far back as they could go, put her head out the window and inhaled for a long time. Only then did she put the Kentucky Fried Chicken bag on the chest of drawers. The lines on her face shortened.

Then she moved to the side of the bed. She lifted her top to adjust her black skirt, making sure the side seams were where they should be. With both hands she pulled her loose black top back over the elastic skirt's waistband. For a minute, her hands caressed her waistline. She sat down at the head of the bed and took off her black sandals, kicking them away from her. Then she put her head in her hands, her elbows on her thighs and sank into a deep silence.

Phatheka opened the Kentucky Fried Chicken bag. "You must be hungry. Let's eat." She checked the time again, attaining the distance she needed between her eyes and the face of the watch.

"Anything yet?" Phatheka's raised voice shook Zaba to attention.

"No, Sis'Phatheka."

"How do you feel?"

"I wish I were feeling as sunny and flowery inside," she sighed, her eyes on the bedcover.

"Child, when all this is over, you will be yourself again."

Phatheka had taken to calling Zaba "child" even though there was a gap of only fifteen years in their ages. When they first met five years ago, Zaba often complained about being called thus. Then Phatheka would say: "Listen child, I was fourteen when I got my first period. I could have been your mother."

They put their food on their laps and ate in silence. When they finished, Phatheka went to the window and reached for the handle. Zaba protested, "Please don't – I won't be able to hold this food in with this paint smell."

Phatheka came back, tidied up the bones and the skin Zaba had taken off her chicken pieces, and put everything in the plastic bag.

"Tea?" Phatheka walked out the bedroom towards the kitchen. The bare walls felt closer to her than they did when first they came to drop their bags. She scanned the walls, yearning for something to look at. Before she went to the kitchen, she peeped into the lounge, her eyes taking in not just the furniture, but each corner of the room, as if she was not convinced they were alone. Once in the kitchen she put on the kettle, then decided to use the toilet.

Behind the door at the other end of the corridor lay transformation. Phatheka was surprised by the changes. Although her cousin Menzi had told her about the renovations, she had not expected this. Menzi had broken down one wall, extending another to create a roomy communal space for private bodily needs. Two toilets stood next to each other to the left. To the right were two shower rooms with white plastic curtains. In the middle, right opposite the door, two sinks, each with a rubbish bin underneath. Two towel rails hung above the sink. The white towels matched the white wall tiles and the ceiling. Above the towel rail, a large window with a white curtain adorned the wall. The floor tiles were royal blue.

The bathroom did not fit with the rest of the house, Phatheka mused. It looked as if it had never been used.

Back in the kitchen, Phatheka boiled the kettle again. She headed back to the bedroom with two mugs and a milk jug on a tray. She noticed that Zaba had placed her folded dressing-gown on the foot of the bed. She had taken out her toilet bag and placed it between the head of the bed and the couch. She was sitting in the same spot on the bed, gazing into the space beyond the drawn curtains that matched the bedcover. She looked up, took the mug Phatheka offered, said thank you with her eyes. She frowned at the first sip, tightening her lips. "O! Sis'Phatheka, it's far too sweet."

"I did that on purpose. You need energy in that body." Phatheka sat on the couch and started sipping.

"Do you feel anything yet?" Phatheka asked without looking at Zaba.

"No."

"My friend is a pro. She says we are all different. It will come. We must be patient."

When they were both finished, Phatheka took the mug from Zaba's hand.

"Child, where does Zaba come from? That's the name you gave her this morning, right?"

"Sis'Phatheka, I'd rather not talk about it. Not now, please."

"OK, another time."

Zaba started to undress. She got her pyjamas from her bag, put them on, and turned to Phatheka, "I know it's too late now, but I really don't like this situation with the shared toilets. How can many people share one toilet?"

"There are two."

"That's not the point. Each bedroom should have its own."

"But this is just a boarding-house."

Zaba was out of the door before Phatheka could finish talking. Phatheka quickly closed the windows, then took her knitting out of her suitcase. Then she took her reading glasses from her handbag and put them on. Next, she got her shawl from her suitcase and placed it over her lap. Just as she had settled back on the couch to knit, Zaba came back in.

"Very clean, right?" Phatheka said with an inviting face. Zaba nodded, headed for the bed. She pulled the blanket up to her ears and then curled her body into what Phatheka thought was an uncomfortable position.

Phatheka smiled as she thought about the numerous occasions she had tried to encourage her friend to "add a bit of fat to that pole". But Zaba simply laughed when

Phatheka said, "For a school principal, you are too thin, child. Someone with such a status should show it in stature."

"Did you bring one of your many books?" Phatheka asked as the knitting needles swished against each other.

"No. I couldn't, Sis'Phatheka."

Phatheka looked at her watch in her usual manner. It read *21:20 FRI.*

She knitted. Now and again she held her work of creation away with arms stretched so she could admire it. She gathered pace with time. She wished there was a bedside lamp so she could dim the light in the room a bit. That way her young friend would get the deep sleep she needed.

When Phatheka opened her eyes, her shawl had fallen to her feet, her glasses hung halfway down her nose. Zaba was already out of bed, gripping her toilet bag in her right hand.

"Is this it?" Phatheka stood up immediately, stepping on her bundle of knitting. She reached Zaba from behind, putting her arms around the body that now felt like a rigid frame. She walked slightly behind her, slightly to her left. When they got to the door, Phatheka opened it and started to edge out.

Zaba said, "Sis'Phatheka, please wait in here. I'll be fine."

She held her midriff with both hands pushed close into herself. The creases on her forehead greeted the floor.

"No, I am coming with you."

"No, Sis'Phatheka," Zaba said in a low voice even while her face, now looking into the other woman's face, screamed. Phatheka remembered the promise she had made as she took a step backwards.

Zaba held onto the wall with one hand as she stepped into the corridor. She took a left turn, four more steps and reached the door of the toilet.

Phatheka's eyes were drawn to the fresh drops of blood on the plastic tiles in the doorway. She stared, unmoving. Then she took a few steps, her eyes bent on tracing subsequent drops of blood to the toilet door. The door was already shut behind Zaba. Then she heard the inner toilet door bang. She wondered which toilet Zaba had chosen. Then she looked at the blood again. The drops began to spread into one another. Phatheka knew she would have to give her friend privacy. She could not follow her to get a cloth to wipe up the blood. If she could wait, so could the blood drops.

Phatheka's watch read: *00:45 SAT*.

She gathered up her knitting and placed it in her suitcase. She took the tray with mugs and the plastic Kentucky Fried Chicken bag to the kitchen. She put the kettle on, threw the plastic bag into the rubbish bin, and rinsed the mugs. Then she walked down the corridor, trying each door handle as she passed. When no door opened, she knew they were all locked. She tried the toilet door. It was locked. She put her left ear against the door, her eyes wide open as if to aid her hearing. She heard nothing. She walked back to the kitchen.

She washed the mugs again, got the tray ready, then paced down the corridor towards the toilet. Her left hand fisted over her pendant watch, right between her breasts. This time she stood with her back flat against the toilet door. When her thighs began to tremble ever so slightly, she paced back to the kitchen.

In the kitchen she did not let go of the watch. By now her fisted hand was deep between her breasts as if to steady herself. With the right hand, she opened drawers and cabinet doors, looked without seeing, shutting them again.

"The nearest telephone is five taxi stops away. It's at my friend's butchery."

Menzi's voice rang in Phatheka's ears at that moment, something she would have preferred not to be reminded of. Voices in her head started whispering: "What if the worst happens?" Just as she thought they were getting too loud to bear, she thought she heard a noise.

She dashed on tiptoe towards the toilet door. Flushing noise. She rushed back to the kitchen, collected the tray, took the kettle as well this time, and went to place these on the chest of drawers. When Zaba re-entered the bedroom, Phatheka was sitting on the couch, her thighs moving repetitively under her shawl, her hands over the shawl.

Zaba's face now looked like something Phatheka could not put into words. In her hands, she cupped a ball of toilet paper. She shuffled in, lowered herself on the bed and then extended her hands to Phatheka. Her eyes fixed on her older friend's outstretched hands, she whispered, "Sisi, please put it there." Her eyes pointed to the chest of drawers. Then she cried. First without making a sound.

Phatheka took the ball of toilet paper, noticing streaks of red in the inner layers, placed it next to the tray, and reached for the bottle of Valium in her handbag. "These helped my husband after his accident. Take them." She reached for the kettle, poured water into the mug and gave the tablets to Zaba. In between her cries, she asked, "What are these for?" She did not wait for an answer before swallowing the tablets, pressing her abdomen down with one hand.

"They kill pain, calm you down and give you sleep. For my husband, they did."

Zaba now held her abdomen with both hands, her fingers digging in. She got under the bedcovers and continued crying.

Phatheka sat on the couch and watched quietly, her left hand just touching the bed. Her head dropped. She kept saying, as if just to herself, "Cry, it's OK," over and over again. She did not know for how long she did this. When at last she realised that Zaba was asleep, she picked up her shawl, placed it over her chest and shoulders, reclined and closed her eyes. She felt as if her mind wanted her to sleep.

When Phatheka felt some movement on the bed again, she knew she had dozed off. She checked her watch: *03:30 SAT.*

Zaba got out of bed slowly, walked to her bag next to the wall, and bent over it for some time. When she rose and turned, she held a lime cigarette lighter, a Coca Cola bottle with a clear liquid, and a plastic sandwich bag. She stood in front of Phatheka.

"Sis'Phatheka, before the sun comes up can you please…" She looked at the ball of toilet paper on the chest of drawers and handed the older woman the lighter, the Coca Cola bottle and the plastic bag.

"What?"

"I want to take it back home."

"No, I can't. I won't. That's…"

"In the garden, I saw this morning. You can do it there."

"Wait, let's think this through…"

"Sis'Phatheka, there's nothing to think through, you promised..."

"You did not speak about doing this. This is not what…"

Zaba put her right finger on her lips and just looked at Phatheka. Phatheka's mind rushed to that day two weeks ago in the principal's office where she had gone to tell Zaba she had thought of a solution that might work. Zaba had looked straight into her eyes, thanked her for making this possible, and asked for support to the very end. Phatheka had absorbed the seriousness on Zaba's face then. She knew she had no choice now. She took a deep breath.

"Child, I will. Now you get back to sleep. Take two more tablets. How's the flow?"

"Thank you, Sis'Phatheka. Yes, I do need to change."

Zaba left the bedroom. Phatheka put the lighter, Coca Cola bottle and plastic sandwich bag next to the ball of toilet paper. When she tried to imagine what the little thing looked like, she felt her stomach move. She went back to the couch and started knitting again. Zaba came back and went to bed.

Phatheka knitted. She felt her fingers go numb. Her eyes felt heavy and sore, but she did not stop. She went to the kitchen to make another cup of tea, then returned to her knitting. After she had gone to the toilet, she went back to knitting. Even when her eyes started watering as she read the pattern book, she simply rubbed them and returned to knitting. Now and again she stood up, moved the curtain aside, looked out. She knitted faster and faster. Zaba lay still, her back to Phatheka, facing the wall, closer to the wall than before.

When dim rays of light found the window, Phatheka stopped knitting. She stood up. She folded the cardigan, put the needles through the folded cardigan, wound the loose thread of wool around each ball, and put these on the couch. She folded the shawl, put it in her suitcase. She put her doek on her head and walked to the chest of drawers. She checked the time: *05:45 SAT*. She took the ball of toilet paper, and what Zaba had given her, then took a breath.

She walked to the kitchen, opened the door leading to the side and back garden, and stepped outside. The air was humid. She looked up and knew the sun would be up soon, no clouds. There was just enough light for her to see in the garden.

She walked through the garden, took in the mixture of smells, and immediately found a spot that seemed right for the job: two rocks, next to each other. She placed the ball of toilet paper where the rocks touched. She opened the Coca Cola bottle and poured what smelt like paraffin over it. Then she lit it. For a second, the flame seemed to come alive; then it died. The toilet paper, now much smaller, black and wet, was stuck to the foetus inside. "This is even smaller than my fist," she thought, realising then that she had expected something bigger, without knowing why.

She tried again. It shrivelled into a smaller, blacker mass. The whiff escaped from the shiny black shrinking mound directly into her nostrils. She felt her insides come together into a ball, then turn, a movement that made her dizzy for a split second. Her jaws tightened in response and locked until they hurt. Her upper lip touched her nose and stayed like that. Her breathing kept getting deeper.

She concentrated on the task at hand. She repeatedly stretched her jaws with a yawn-like movement, then tightened them again. When finally it became clear to her that she was not going to get the ash Zaba needed to take back home, she decided on a different route, trusting that Zaba would understand.

She looked towards the back of the garden, noticed a fleshy fern. Using the plastic sandwich bag as a glove, she gathered the shrunken foetus and dug a hole with her bare hands close to the fern. She buried it, wrapped in the plastic sandwich bag, close to the bark so that it could be in the shade for all time. Back at the rocks, she collected the empty Coca Cola bottle and the lighter. She walked to the house.

When Phatheka returned to the bedroom after washing her hands, Zaba was sitting up on the bed, supporting her back with two pillows. Zaba waited until Phatheka had sat down on her couch, after removing her doek, folding it and placing it on her suitcase.

Once Phatheka had settled, Zaba asked, "What was it?"

"I don't know."

"Didn't you look?"

"No, I couldn't." Phatheka looked down with her hands on her face.

Zaba responded with tears. She cried without changing her position.

After what seemed like eternity for Phatheka, Zaba asked again.

"Can I at least see the ashes. I just want to…"

"No. I couldn't." After a long pause she continued, "I buried it."

Zaba started to cry aloud, her body the choreography of agony. Phatheka offered her tissues.

Amidst the cries, Phatheka heard Zaba say, "I just wanted to take her home with me." That made Phatheka move. She went and sat on the bed next to Zaba, held her firmly. Phatheka wept more quietly.

When Zaba's voice subsided, Phatheka let her go, went to her handbag for more tablets and offered them to Zaba, who was now using the bed sheet to wipe her tears and blow her nose. She took the tablets without a word, then lay down facing the wall.

Phatheka went back to her couch, unravelled her knitting and tried to knit. She fell asleep from an exhaustion she had been unaware of just a second before.

When Phatheka opened her eyes again, the sun was streaming through the open curtains. Zaba sat on the bed in clean day clothes – a pair of black denim pants and a loose grey T-shirt. Her face looked like the dawn of another day.

"Oh, what time is it?" Phatheka asked, rubbing her eyes and stretching.

"Hmm, 9.30. I've just made us some tea," Zaba said as she stood up to hand Phatheka her mug.

"Thank you."

"Sis'Phatheka, I think we should leave today."

"No, we are booked until Monday."

"Oh, I forgot. It's a long weekend."

"That's why we chose it."

"No, Sis'Phatheka, you chose it."

"Yes, I did." She sighed, bored her eyes into Zaba's eyes, and spoke slowly, "Because, my child, even the sun needs enough time to rise."

Zaba looked at Phatheka and smiled, her small eyes almost closing.

"Thank you, Sisi, but who is going to look after your shop?"

"I took care of that. My son is a man now. I'm learning to trust him."

A warm silence fell between the two women. Their faces began to thaw. The air around mimicked their faces.

"How's the knitting going? I've never seen you in those colours. Aren't those too bright for you?"

"It's not mine, it's my daughter's."

As Phatheka said this, the sticky stench of burning flesh, paraffin, fresh blood and moist toilet paper welled up in her nose. She clenched her jaws, hoping to blow the smell away. She looked at her feet. In 48 years she had never smelled anything like it.

Phatheka folded her knitting, stood up and walked towards the door.

"What do you think is best? Dying before you have been given a name or afterwards?"

"Child, this is why we need time. We have to talk. About everything."

The Odds of Dakar

"I REMEMBER THIS NAME," the woman at the registration table says. "Nomandla. When I lived in New York I used to join all the South African rallies and demonstrations; we boycotted South African products…"

These kinds of comments have become familiar to me. I have heard them so many times, often when I travel. But somehow I am unprepared for them when the woman at the registration table looks at my form, reads my name out loud and starts talking to me. I listen to her reminiscences and then watch as she burst out singing "Nkosi sikelel' iAfrica" I want to ask her if she is Senegalese, why she had been in New York and for how long and why she is sitting behind a table at this grand hotel in Dakar. To the left of the registration table is a table for another conference, with two much younger-looking women sitting and talking, no one to attend to. Instead of satisfying my curiosity, I look at the woman's name tag pinned on a soft deep purple jacket. I smile, mumble something about the bygone days of struggle, try to pronounce her name as I thank her and rush off to my room. I need to be outside, to feel the air on my cheeks; I want to take a quick walk before the welcome session begins at four.

How could I have known that Nomandla would spoil my plan like this? I wanted to travel as a shawl, that pale pink wide pashmina that she was given for her fortieth birthday. She hates it: the colour, the fabric, the width. I completely fail to understand what could be so objectionable about the width of a shawl. I get the colour thing. I also dislike some colours. The difference is I have no reason to object with such emotion; it's a waste of energy. Fabric choice is crucial; I agree with her there: clothes need to hug, embrace, comfort, and cuddle while they look good and fit well. Accessories should do all that with additional verve. After all, they are dispensable. She says this shawl is far too wide; it should not be hanging so low over her arms.

I have asked myself many times why she has not given it away to someone who would adore it, but then I know the answer to that question; she doesn't believe in giving away gifts. She keeps them all, the old, the ugly, the useless and the cheap. She has kept this shawl over a decade. I have watched her pack this shawl on her travels many times and never use it once. At home, where she has many more to choose from, she hardly ever lifts it from the drawer. A month ago, when she went to London, I chose to travel as that black cotton and raw silk smart-casual jacket. Big mistake. She wouldn't take me off, from morning to midnight, for formal meetings, dinners and casual evening jols, she would not change. I caught her a few times talking to herself, wondering why she needed to wear the jacket one more time, then finding the perfect reason, the only reason she needed: it matched whatever clothes she wore. That's why I wanted to travel as her least favourite shawl; I needed peace. And, now, the first thing she is taking out of her suitcase is the pale-pink pashmina. Me.

There's a knock on the door and I quickly answer. Brother V stands smiling, a boyish grin of anticipation.

"Shall we?"

"Yep, what colour shall we paint Dakar?" I ask as I drape my shawl. We arrived at the crack of dawn and now I feel energised after a light lunch.

"All we have time for is a quick walk around the hotel. The session starts at four, remember?"

I look at my watch: it is after three. "And some fresh Atlantic ocean air," I suggest. Do you think the salt might smell different?"

"What nonsense … sea salt is sea salt everywhere."

"That's not true sea sand is different everywhere. I know; I collect it. The colour, the texture, the size of the grain; it is never ever the same."

As we walk to the stretch of the coastline I had seen from my window, we talk inanely about the seas of the world and their waters. Travelling together or in the office, Brother V and I talk nonsense with such seriousness, trying to forget, I suppose, the seriousness of our lives and work. I notice for the first time, though, that we both love the sea. There is a twinkle in his eyes.

I am beginning to really like this man, Brother V as we call him. He is just a few months older than me; we feel comfortable in each other's company; we share similar ideas about life and politics. When we do differ, it is fiercely, and often on two issues – well two sides of the same issue really – white guilt and white privilege. There is a warmth and caring that comes out of his heart that does not match his outer appearance. That chest seems to carry empathy in large doses, available on demand.

The other reason I chose to travel as a shawl is that I hate the sea. I wanted to hide, to rest at the bottom of Nomandla's suitcase, where she likes layering the thick shawls, gowns and towels when she packs. I like the dark; it feeds me. It keeps my imagination alive, my senses pulsating. I hate that ocean smell; that never-ending blueness of incessantly moving water makes my head spin. I hate it when it's windy and the sand blinds me. Shells and rocks make me see double and triple. Slimy water-creatures are downright unsightly. She has now folded me tightly around her neck. There is a nip in the air.

"It's not that cold."

"Oh shut up!" I tighten my shawl and lift some of it to cover my ears.

"I want to see the pool, feel how warm it is. Maybe I'll swim."

"In this weather?"

"Later, when it warms up a bit. We'll go to the beach straight afterwards."

I stride to catch up with Brother V, who is taking one step for every two of mine. Then I stop dead and turn.

"What's wrong?" Brother V is looking into my face. A lone female form in the distance has also stopped. It is as if we turned at the same time. Far away as she is, she knows it is me, just as I know it is her. She climbs over a short hedge and comes towards us.

"Who is that?" Brother V asks. My face must look terribly troubled to make his voice so anxious. I know my mouth has dried up, and I imagine it must be open. I watch as the woman approaches.

"Who is it?"

"My ex," I explain. "The one who dumped me by email." I know my voice is shaking. So is my body.

Brother V looks at me again. "What should I–?"

"Just don't go anywhere, please."

Now she is right in front of us. Brother V steps to the side, just one step. I shoot a look at his tall frame that says: did you not hear me? Don't move, I said.

How could I have known I needed to avoid this as well! I know her, that water-loving lover of hers, the one who swims like a shark and surfs like a man. Who started her on that ridiculous sand-collecting hobby. I never liked her. There was always something about her: intangible yet palpable. She seemed to lose touch with her core every now and again. Who can trust that? I suppose I shouldn't lie: I did like Lucille, just a little, at the beginning. That was way back, seven years ago. That smile, those teeth, those eyes … and those days when I was close to Nomandla's body… even I could feel her love at the slightest touch.

She is standing in front of us, smiling, saying, "Hi." I count at least seven colours in circular shapes on her jacket. It fits comfortably around her shoulders. She looks good, slimmer.

"Hi," I say, making sure my feet are firm on the ground. I am not smiling. The pain that has been hidden at the bottom of my heart for six months starts to fill my chest. For a moment I think I might collapse. So I dig my feet into the grass, the ground soft and damp from rain. I fix my eyes on her face, pretending to be still inside.

She reaches her hand out to Brother V. "My name is Lucille."

He shakes her hand, then looks at me as if to say: What next?

"How long are you here?" she asks me.

Push her into the pool, stupid. Brother V, help her! You know the story. Who does she think she is? Dakar is not her city; what kind of question is that? How could that be an appropriate first thing to say after you dumped someone via email, without any explanation, and never followed up, except to cancel the plans you had made? This is when I truly hate being an invisible sense. What is the point if Nomandla can't even hear me?

I remember the day so clearly. I had begun with ease and was full of anticipation – just the way Fridays should begin. I was on her reading glasses, where I prefer to be on ordinary working days. I'd like to believe I help her more that way as she has so much reading and writing to do in her office. She may not admit it, but when she has to make those tough decisions, I guide her through them all.

I heard the question clearly and I know the answer, but I am lost. I am trying to figure out what Lucille is doing here on the edge of Africa, my continent. I remember the second registration table in the hotel lobby, and recall the name of their conference. What sort of person would attend that conference? "The Research for Policy and Advocacy Initiative: Strengthening Community-Based Organisations

Working Towards the Reduction and Eventual Eradication of Maternal Mortality and Morbidity in English-Speaking Countries of the Sub-Saharan Region of the African Continent." People should be more creative, I think; what a ridiculous name for a conference.

"Two days," I answer at last. I don't tell her that I won't be able to see Gorée Island; I have had to cut my stay short by a whole day so that I can be back home to watch my daughter's play. It's the first play she has scripted and directed, and I'm not missing that for anything. Tomorrow I will present my paper and then leave, praying that my flight lands on time. Two days, and what is it to you, anyway?

I said: push her into the pool, and let's see what questions she can muster once she is in there, her fancy jacket wet as rain. I can't believe you'll let Lucille get away with this. Have you forgotten those emailed words? "I feel that for me, you and I would better be suited as friends than love partners." That was only six months ago.

"This isn't easy," she says, her eyes on me. I stare back at her, feeling deep down in my bones that I do not wish to touch her or talk to her. I do not even wish to see her face. I turn, look Brother V in the eye, and say with as much control as I can muster, "Shall we go?"

Lucille steps aside, and we walk away. It feels as if my knees are loosening, as if I cannot trust myself to continue walking. My whole body begins to shake slightly.

"Please hold me."

Without a word, Brother V comes close and puts a long arm around my shoulders. I hold my head still, making sure I do not look back, that I keep walking away, one step at a time. Brother V towers over me, and I am grateful he is so tall.

What an opportunity missed. Instead of saying what she really felt, she answered Lucille's questions like a little girl. Instead of hurling every insult she ever knew, she lost her voice and walked away. Lucille will never respect her after this; she failed to show her just who she is. Even that Brother V of hers was just pathetic, standing there, holding out his hand to greet the bitch. As if he didn't remember her tears, her sadness, the pain embedded in her marrow. Why did he just stand there? He should have testified what it took for Nomandla to recover, how long he had to hold her together. He should have told her. That moment will never be repeated, and she missed it. Him too.

The further away from the pool we walk, the more I feel as if my skin will peel off my body. I feel naked and raw. I want to scream and go back to strangle her. I wonder what Brother V thinks of me. He must be very disappointed in me. But I don't care what he thinks; I am just so glad I did not wish to touch her. I had no desire to lay my head on her chest. I did not even see her lips. Strange, that: it was as if she were talking through a simple gap; those lips were gone. The spark had vanished. The magic had disappeared.

"You handled that very well. I'm impressed."

"You think so?"

"I would have thrown her into the swimming-pool."

Why didn't you? Even I think you should have.

"It's a real pity we can't go to Gorée Island."

I look up at Brother V as I speak, and he knows I don't want to talk about the encounter. I circle my left hand around his waist, hold tight. I wonder what we must look like to onlookers. We walk along the edge. There is no beach to speak of, wild groundcover sprawled everywhere amid ill-formed rocks. My friend Priya would have known the botanical name of this ground cover. She is the only activist I know who loves plants and studies them as a hobby.

You can look back now. She's gone now, back to the main building of the hotel. If you listen to me from now on, I will make sure you never bump into her again.

"Ever read Senghor's poetry?" This just comes out as I am thinking of Priya, not because I want a conversation.

"No, why? He is Senegalese, right?" I feel Brother V's eyes on the crown of my head, but I do not want to look up at his face, for him to see how the encounter with Lucille has unsettled me.

"What are the odds?"

"What?" he asks.

Now I lift my eyes to face him as we walk on. "I still can't believe what just happened."

That's your problem: thinking ahead is not your strength. There's no going back now.

"There was a woman at the registration table who told me she was in the anti-apartheid movement in New York. Did you ever live there?"

"I wish."

"You might know her. Maybe she lived in London or the Netherlands. She looked worldly."

"What does worldly look like?" He teases. "Maybe she knows your Lucille. She's from New York, right?"

Lucille was never in the anti-apartheid movement in New York or anywhere else. She is just an American.

It occurs to me then that I have spent most of this walk with my head lowered to the ground and my eyes on my feet. It's warmer. I look out to sea and try to find something to focus on. The path takes us around the hotel grounds and is curving gently back towards the main entrance. We are now approaching the golf course, about to walk past people for the first time since we set out. Brother V's hold on my shoulder loosens. Gradually, the golfers come to come into view. I look up and see my third-floor room, where I have left the balcony doors open.

Does this not remind of the balcony at the Durban Bluff that day you had just reconciled with Lucille, when you had a house to yourselves and she loved you differently? I was your daytime moisturiser. You used to sit on the sand and watch her swim. You took photograph upon photograph of her in that turquoise bathing costume. The two of you made love before breakfast with the sun shining on your bodies in the lounge. You ate nuts and dried fruits and drank water and herb tea. You sat on the floor and read aloud to each other. You joined sunset watchers for dinner at that restaurant every afternoon. You never exchanged a word of disagreement.

Brother V bends over to pick up a ball and starts a conversation with one of the golfers. I follow the path back to the entrance. I take one more look at the sea, then the trees and the tennis court. Just as I begin to wonder where Brother V is, I feel his hands on my shoulders.

"How are you feeling?"

"Better, thanks."

"I think we need to speed up; our session starts in five minutes."

So many opportunities missed in a single hour. What are the odds? She doesn't listen to a single suggestion I make.

The Suit Continued:
The Other Side

IT'S TIME. ALL these years I've watched quietly, listened silently, to one side of the story. I've travelled far and wide, watched and listened from convenient spots on walls. I've seen the expressions on people's faces. They all scorned me. They all thought I was a cheat, ungrateful. They seemed to want to spit at me from their seats in every single theatre I visited in. No one, not one person, ever asked the question: if Matilda were here today, what would she tell us?

This young chap Siphiwo Mahala – so far he is the only one who seems able to think out of the box, as the young people like to say these days. He at least sat and thought, and he realised there has never been only one way to slaughter a cow. But then he took Terence's side, because even in his eyes and mind I was the devil herself. If I must be honest – as this is truth-time – it was Siphiwo who gave me the idea to come out and speak for myself. I have always known that one day I would have to speak out loud, but he made me think that now is in fact a good time. He wrote that piece – and then I knew I had to tell my side of the story: now or never. That way, the world will know the truth and I can finally rest.

My mother used to like saying "the truth is always more complicated than the lie, my child". May your bones rest in peace, Mama. I know you are listening. May you be proud of me. I'll start at the beginning: Gladys.

Gladys always stood out. She raised her deep voice only when she sang. She liked Sophie Mgcina's songs. She sang them casually, spontaneously at the shebeens. Sometimes people asked her to sing and she obliged. I liked the way she came alive when she sang. Her eyebrows lifted as if to kiss her hairline, her eyes opened wider and wider, and she smiled a smile that said, "I am here". Some people said although her voice was not as good as Sophie's, her stage presence was more vibrant, more engaging. She was always more relaxed than Sophie; you could say she performed without it looking as if she was putting on an act. I liked that. We were not friends then, she was just a woman whose voice and performance I enjoyed. That was when I was still single.

Gladys disappeared. People said she went away to try her luck in music, as women who had talent often did in those days. Sophiatown was not the place for talented women. No one ever said *where* she went for this luck-fishing expedition. Some said she went to find a husband in the land of amaShangane. They said she was in Lourenço Marques. I missed her voice. I met and married Philemon.

I saw her again at the House of Spirits after three years. No one had told me she was back in Sophiatown. I was there with Philemon, as the *Drum* boys were having a party.

I don't remember whose birthday party it was, but like most parties, people gathered at Can Themba's House of Spirits, and did what they did best. When Philemon said we must go, I put on my best dress and some perfume he had bought me.

We had not been there long when I heard Gladys's distinct voice.

"Matty, there you are," she said as if we had just spoken a few minutes ago. She smiled, opened her arms and drew me close to her chest as if she had really missed me. Most people called me Tilly, but to her I was Matty. Had always been Matty even during those casual encounters. The only other person who called me that was Mama, bless her soul.

"Want some fresh air?" She did not give me time to respond, telling Philemon "I'll bring her back. We need to talk, stay with your men friends." Philemon smiled and waved goodbye with his left hand, his right tight around his glass.

I did not say a word as we walked out, weaving our way through jiving groups of people, swaying couples and drunks, to the fresh dark outside. The sky was the deep, deep blue of Sophiatown winters. Only the stars seemed to be aware of us. Gladys held my hand and led the way around corners and walls. Now and again a fowl jumped out from nowhere and ran away, a dog barked at us, a child disappeared around a corner – but not an adult soul came our way. As I was getting ready to ask where she was taking me, I was leaning with my back against a wall, her breasts upon mine, her eyes like stars shining into mine. My surprise was not stronger than the electricity that began to run through my body. Gladys moved swiftly yet smoothly. Her lips on mine pushed away even the suggestion of a question that had tried to formulate itself in my head – or was it in my heart – a second earlier. I trembled without knowing why. The pleasure was as profound, and as undeniable as the change that that moment set in motion for the remainder of my life.

In time I learned things about this new world I never could have imagined. Sophiatown became a new place. How could I have lived so blindly, so deafly, yet so passionlessly before? Gladys introduced me to corners and slopes of Sophiatown I did not know existed. She did the same with my body, my mind, my worldview. Astoundingly, the rest of Sophiatown remained blinkered. Even on days when Gladys went home in broad daylight, after we had left no inch of each other's bodies untouched, Sophiatown remained Sophiatown, where people saw only what they want to see.

The only people we avoided like lice were the *Drum* boys. We chose our meeting places carefully. The House of Spirits was never one of them. People said the *Drum* boys smelled stories from a distance. They said journalists are born not made, they sense the stories as they unfold. They only go to the scene to confirm them. That's what people said about Henry Nxumalo in particular. They said he had dreams about events before they occurred. Many people were afraid of his powers. Some even said he had been sent to Johannesburg to perform his magic by his

Zulu ancestors because Johannesburg needed this kind of magic.

I was living a life I had never imagined would be mine, a smaller Sophiatown inside the bigger Sophiatown. Gladys introduced me to all her smaller Sophiatown friends. What I had never told even my closest friends was that Philemon had never taken me from the front. We had discussed this. I really thought myself lucky, a man who was in no rush to prove his manhood by making me pregnant! We agreed it was the only form of contraception that guaranteed no pregnancy. I wanted to wait until we could give our children more, much more than what we had got from our parents. Philemon told me he was not sure about ever becoming a father. That was his reason for waiting. But I hoped that in time, he would change his mind. I told Gladys about this soon after we started our own thing. She was the first and last person I ever told. Gladys, however, had an illuminating take on my version of the story.

Another page in the book of my Sophiatown opened to me.

About six months after the night of the deep blue sky and seeing stars, Philemon said to me, "That Gladys makes you happy, Tilly, I can see."

I smiled and said, "Your journalist makes you happy too." I watched shock rush across his face, quickly replaced by composure. I was so glad Gladys and I had shared that secret. It was a relief when those words came to me. Philemon and I signed and sealed a contract in silence. That was the last day we touched in bed.

A year from the night of the deep blue sky and bright stars, Gladys told me our relationship needed to "change for the better". When I asked her what that meant, she said we had to leave Sophiatown and go and live somewhere far away, like East London or Port Elizabeth or Durban, where our relationship could be open – or should I say, less closed. I could see that she had started resenting the fact that I was married to Philemon. But what was I supposed to do? We were not supposed to have been, in those days. Some of her friends in the smaller Sophiatown lived lives of constant uncertainty and fear of rejection. On the other hand, I had never left Sophiatown. I could not imagine living in places I had only ever heard of. How could I leave Sophiatown?

"Matty, I am not just your friend, as Stupid Sophiatown likes to believe."

I can never forget those words, in the same way that I can never forget the frustrations they brought.

How could I leave Philemon? How could I divorce him? He was so kind to me. Many Sophiatownians said how lucky I was to have a man who treated me like a queen. Some said I had bewitched him, because no black man in those days treated his wife like that.

Gladys became impatient – it felt like overnight – but to be fair, she was patient at first. She was so patient that I started to think about the possibility of a life outside of Sophiatown. Gladys was good at making me see things differently. That's just who she was. Being a teacher, persuasion probably came easy to her.

But then we started to fight. At first, it was over little things. Soon she threatened to tell my mother-in-law, my friends, my neighbours, the whole of Sophiatown, about us. I was confused, disappointed. I felt trapped. We saw less and less of each other. Then one day, Gladys greeted me with an unexpected smile and launched in.

"Matty, I have a plan. You said you like children. You just wanted to delay their coming. I don't mind children. Pregnancy. Pregnancy is our only way out of this conundrum." Gladys then laid out to me the whole plan as she had conceived it.

The silent contract Philemon and I had was to remain sealed. Once pregnancy occurred, Philemon would feel less exposed by releasing me. Gladys and I chose Terence. He taught at the same school as Gladys, and she knew him well. Gladys said she would absent herself on D-day. I liked this plan.

Seducing Terence at Thirty Nine Steps was as easy as Gladys had said it would. Internally I was uncomfortable, but I kept my eyes on the goal. I imagined Durban – a house tucked under a rock facing the beach. Warmth, humidity and ever-fresh air. Gladys, the baby and me.

Terence was like dough in my hands. After Gladys, I could never enjoy the sex but again, I kept my vision alive. Durban became real to me.

Gladys and I discussed names. We agreed on unisex names. We had a list of five that we planned to start narrowing down once I became pregnant. I still remember them all: Kwenzekile, Langalethu, S'mamukelisiwe,

Kusasalethu and Sisonke. We wanted the name to capture our situation with tenderness.

Once our plan was in motion, Gladys calmed down. Our fights stopped. A new pattern emerged; Gladys and I would not see each other for at least three days after I had been with Terence.

Three months later we were still trying. Terence seemed to like me. Trying was less and less of a chore as time passed, but I was getting sick of it.

Then disaster struck: Radio Maphikela broadcast the news about me and Terence. I saw a vengeful side of Philemon I never knew existed. Gladys explained it to me. She said Philemon was afraid that now I was going out with other men, he would be exposed. Making me do that thing with the suit was his defense mechanism.

"Sophiatown is still Sophiatown," said Gladys. I did not ask exactly what she meant. She said everything would pass, and I should just focus on our goal. I did.

What Can Themba could not have known about that day Philemon made me carry the suit down Ray Street is that as we passed the Anglican Mission of Christ the King, Gladys appeared from nowhere. First I felt her presence. Then I saw her out the corner of my eye. I turned. Our eyes met for a brief second before she hurried on. I was aware of her all the way. She did not take her eyes from us. When we turned into Main Road, I felt her turn too. She stayed on the opposite side of the road. It made me want to cry.

Philemon could see my pain, but I doubt he saw Gladys. I think he was just so pleased with himself in his own crooked way. Focus, I kept telling myself. Focus, Matilda, focus! We strode up Toby Street and I could see Gladys keeping step on the other side. When we turned into Edward Road, Gladys was still with us. We turned for home and she walked on down the road. I went straight to the bedroom and cried myself to sleep. Philemon did not say a word to me. At suppertime I made sure I put the suit in its place before I even put the food on the table, so he had no reason at all to speak to me.

Gladys did not come to see me for two weeks. It took everything I had to walk to her school gate and wait for her there. I knew this would madden her because we had agreed that once we started the "T-plan" (as we called our design for our future), I would never go to the school. Gladys did not like seeing me with Terence, even though this was her original idea. All I wanted was to hear her voice. I wanted to hear how she felt when she saw me – suit on hanger – walking beside Philemon. I was tired of imagining what she was going through. I had to hear her say it, whatever it was. I stood looking away from the gate, as I could not bear watching Gladys walk towards me. I knew her gait so well, and when I heard her voice, I was ready.

"Matty, didn't we agree…"

"I just couldn't…"

"Let's go to Thirty Nine Steps."

We walked in silence. We both responded to people who greeted us as we walked by. Gladys kept her hands tightly behind her as she walked, her briefcase in them. She took long strides, sometimes leaving me behind. She did not look at me once until we arrived at Thirty Nine Steps. We sat for what felt like eternity without speaking. I did not know where to start. We ordered drinks. I had many things to say. Most of all I wanted to tell her that I still had our goal in mind. As a highly pregnant young woman delivered our order, the tray seemingly resting on her belly, Gladys stood and said she would be back. But I finished my drink and Gladys did not return. I paid for both of us and left.

That suppertime was one of those when I put the suit on the chair before I put the plates on the table. How had all of this happened? My life was suddenly like a bioscope: Philemon, Gladys, Terence, and all the stories I was hearing about Grace, Terence's wife. Here I was alone, very alone. All the plans dispersed in the air. Our vision gone with the Sophiatown storms.

Days later, it occurred to me that I should not give up. Even if Gladys had given up on us, I was not going to. I devised a plan. I needed to look happy, be occupied, so I could attract Gladys back into my life. I called it the Getting Gladys Back plan, GBB for short. I chose to speak to Philemon on a day when he seemed relaxed, reading his newspaper. Now that I knew why he liked *Zonk* newspaper, I understood that he was in a different world when he read it. He looked engaged and happy. When I saw him like this, I knew that Gladys was right.

"Philemon, I'd like to join the married women's cultural club," I announced. He agreed without arguing. He said hopefully this would to stop me "moping around" all day.

The women of the cultural club welcomed me. My life changed. I was moving on to the second part of my GGB. The functions kept my mind occupied. I know Siphiwo Mahala wrote that only three weeks passed between that day that started the solemn saga of the suit and the day they gathered around me, but I know that's not true. It was much longer. Of course he wrote it like that because he was on Terence's side.

One day I walked into the church vestry where the club was meeting to plan a fête and nearly fell over. Gladys was there. No one had told me we had a new member on the planning committee.

"Matty, I was just saying to everyone that it really doesn't make sense that single women like me are excluded from this club. What's the logic? Can *you* maybe tell me?" Gladys looked up at me, and so did the rest of the women.

I missed a step, greeted everyone shyly, and found a corner to sit. We all sat on cushions, the same ones worshippers sat on during the sermons. No one spoke. I was unsure about the mood in the room. It felt somewhat tight without being tense. I swallowed. I smiled. Instinctively I reached for a glass of water and drank. Still no one spoke.

"Gladys, I have been meaning to ask the same question myself. But I am still new in this club, so I was waiting for an opportune moment to ask."

"Think about it, I am three years older than you, right? The only difference is that you are married and I am not. How do you know that tomorrow your club won't tell you that because you don't have a child, they can no longer accept your membership card? What will you do then, Matty?"

Silence reigned. I started to feel the sweat between my breasts. Someone pushed the door further open, and repositioned the brick-sized stone that held it in place. I tried to think, but my mind was blank. Here was an opportunity for me to impress Gladys, and I could not think of a single word!

Gladys spoke again, her voice as calm as the Durban breeze.

"I teach your children, as you all know," she said, and scanned every single woman's face before she continued. "Is this what you want me to teach them? Shall I teach them that married women are a different class of women, and so they need to organise separately? Help me out here, people. What should I tell your children about your club? Better still, what do *you* tell your children about this club?"

Gladys's voice, the Durban breeze on a hot summer day. I began to picture her in class. Then I saw her as a mother. Then I smelled the sea. Then I saw the three of us picking shells. I felt moist sand between my toes. Then I heard myself ask, "What would it take to change this?"

"Nothing," said Mrs Gayiya. She was sitting right next to me. I turned to her. She was smiling. I saw total conviction in her eyes. Her voice was slightly louder than usual.

"Nothing at all. In fact, it's not written down anywhere, Miss Gladys. You got me thinking there. Let's just do it. *We* can do it." The pace of her voice was slightly faster than usual.

The other four members of the planning committee agreed. They said they would lobby the chairman of the club. In those days, women still called themselves chairmen. Gladys asked to be excused, and thanked us for letting her come uninvited and for having listened to her. As she stepped out of the vestry I half stood up, thinking I should see her off. Then I thought that might look silly, and reconnected my behind to my cushion. Before we discussed our plans for that day, we spoke more about Gladys's challenge. She had made us take action. The women said she was a powerful teacher, that's why she had this effect.

In no time, four single women had joined our club. I knew only one of them. She taught at Gladys's school. She was the only one who had always insisted on using her isiZulu name, Nomagugu. I liked her for her daring attitude. In those days, it was hard for black people to claim their mother-tongue names. The story on the streets of Sophiatown was that she had fought really hard with the principal, refusing to give him her Christian name for his register. People said she even threatened to resign. The principal bent the rules, albeit grudgingly.

When Gladys came to club meetings, she avoided me. I was so painfully aware of this. I did not have enough courage to confront her, let alone in front of all those women. I concentrated on the ultimate goal and allowed her to give me the cold shoulder, knowing that my day would come, a day when she would melt in my hands like Zulu mottos melt in your mouth.

I worked hard so I could gain respect from all the others. When I felt that most of them had accepted me, I moved onto to my next step. First I spoke to Philemon. Then I told the women. The next meeting was to be at my home. Some women were excited about meeting Philemon. Others said they just wanted to see us together because we represented the ideal couple.

For days leading to the big event, I was excited. I was also extra-nice to Philemon. I did the suit thing diligently so that he could find it in his heart not to embarrass me in front of my women's club and their husbands. I planned to cook my best never-fail recipes to impress Gladys. I had never really had an opportunity to cook a full meal for her in all this time. When she came to visit during our stolen moments after she finished school and before Philemon's return from work, we often drank our passion and did not need food.

I will not go through the details of that disastrous day. Can Themba gave it to the world to know and to regurgitate and analyse ad nauseum, with me as the villain the whole time. What I want to tell you is my side of my ending. Well, that's what the Sophiatown earthlings saw. I like to think of it as my transition.

When Philemon made me do the suit thing, I was not only surprised, I was disappointed. I realised that I had lived with him all this time without ever knowing him properly. I grinned and bore it. I avoided Gladys's eyes, but focused on the goal. I made myself smell the sea. I saw the waves. I felt humidity on my skin, my hair. I breathed deeply, in and out. I may not have looked calm, but inside I felt as calm as the shells waiting to be picked.

When the visitors were leaving, Gladys lingered in the kitchen. Philemon was outside, saying his goodbyes to the visitors, his voice reflecting his high spirits.

Gladys stood next to the stove and looked straight into my eyes, her arms tightly held under her small firm breasts.

"Matty, I came to say goodbye," she started.

"What…"

"I take the train to Salisbury tomorrow. I am going to live in Rhodesia."

Words evaporated. I watched her walk towards the door and disappear without even trying to touch me. I stood at the door and continued to watch as she hastened her pace. Her black ankle-length skirt swung with her legs as if to help them move faster. As she vanished, the colour of her skirt enveloped my being.

Acknowledgments

Five of these stories were written during the first year of study for the MA in Writing at the University of the Witwatersrand. These stories benefited from feedback from classmates, the course co-ordinator Dr Michael Titlestad and his co-lecturers Lesley Cowling and Dr Ashleigh Harris and Ivan Vladislavić, who was invited to read our stories and give individual feedback.

I am grateful to members of my writing group: Hannelie de Klerk, Vossie Goosen, Lindiwe Nkutha and Yulinda Noortman who provided writerly support and encouragement during that period.

"Running" won the Deon Hofmeyr Award for Creative Writing in 2005 and was later published in *Dinaane: Short Stories by South African Women* (edited by Maggie Davey, Telegram Books, 2007). "Inside" first appeared in *Open: An Erotic Anthology* by South African Women Writers (Oshun Books, 2008). "The Odds of Dakar" first appeared in *Home Away: 24 hours 24 cities 24 writers* (edited by Louis Greenberg, Zebra Press, 2010).

At the launch of *Words Gone Too Soon: A Tribute to Phaswane Mpe and K. Sello Duiker* in Grahamstown in 2005, I was fascinated by the pieces of writing in the book. Most intriguing was Siphiwo Mahala's short story "The Suit Continued". As soon as I finished reading it, my mind began to race. It raced so fast that "The Suit Continued: The Other Side" was written and complete in my head before the festival ended. Naturally, the first thing I did when I arrived back home was to empty my head. About two months later, "Behind The Suit" began brewing in my head and again, I responded. Thank you, Siphiwo, for giving me the idea and the inspiration for the two stories.

Many moons later I read Zukiswa Wanner's "The Dress That Fed The Suit" in *Baobab* and smiled. When Siphiwo's book, *African Delights*, was published in 2011, I read "The Lost Suit" with curiosity. I wonder what Can Themba would have thought of this legacy. Maybe it's time for an anthology of short stories with the title: *The Suit and the Stories it Inspired*.

Thank you Colleen for letting the rain fall on *Running* and for delivering Helen Moffett, with whom I had fun pruning and weeding.

Other fiction titles by Modjaji Books

One Green Bottle
by Debrah Anne Nixon

Shooting Snakes
by Maren Bodenstein

Love Interrupted
by Reneilwe Malatji

Bom Boy
by Yewande Omotoso

Snake
by Tracey Farren

Whiplash
by Tracey Farren

Go Tell the Sun
by Wame Molefe

The Bed Book of Short Stories
edited by Joanne Hichens

This Place I Call Home
by Meg Vandermerwe

The Thin Line
by Arja Salafranca

www.modjajibooks.co.za